O9-AID-676
SAM
THE
CAT
DETECTIVE

Other Apple Paperbacks you will enjoy:

The Adventures of Boone Barnaby
by Joe Cottonwood
Swimmer
by Harriet May Savitz
Fast-Talking Dolphin
by Carson Davidson
Shoebag
by Mary James

LINDA STEWART

SCHOLASTIC INC.
New York Toronto London Auckland Sydney

ISBN 0-590-46145-1

12 11 10 9 8 7 6 5 4 3 2 3 4 5 6 7 8/9

Printed in the U.S.A. 40

First Scholastic printing, February 1993

SAM
THE
CAT
DETECTIVE

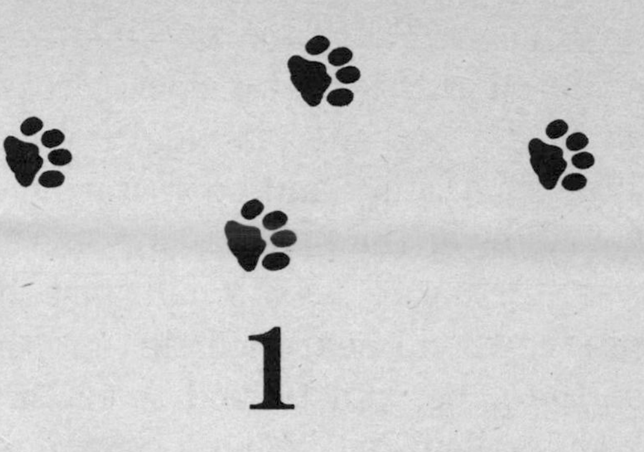

1

It was one of those wet-hot nights in July when living in New York is like living in a teapot. The guy I share my office with had left at five o'clock, after pulling all his usual five o'clock tricks — turning off the air conditioner, turning off the lights, so that seven minutes later I could turn them back on. We go through this every summer. Hunnicker, it has to be reported, is cheap. But then on the other hand, he doesn't charge me rent and I despise petty fights, so we play our little game.

That part aside, we get along pretty well: I stay out of his hair; he stays out of my fur. Hunnicker runs his bookstore from ten to six daily (noon to five Sunday) and I run my agency from six (or five) on.

At least usually I do. Trouble is the private eye trade's been in a slump, and all I'd been running for the last couple of weeks had been Hunnicker's air conditioner. That, and my mouth.

I squinted at the digital clock across the room. It was nearly eight-thirty, and my only activity for three solid hours had been staring out the big front window at the street.

I was starting to chew a nail, just to break the monotony, when I heard a little tentative scratching on the pane, and turned to see a longhaired black-and-yellow girl, about a year-and-a-half old, very slim, very shy. She was looking at me slowly out of troubled blue eyes. She was my kind of trouble. I flicked up my tail and took my foot out of my mouth.

There's a wide brass mail slot at the bottom of the front door — another good reason why I chose this address — and I motioned for her to enter.

She landed on the welcome mat and offered me a slightly offended little pout. "You treat all your customers like third-class mail?"

"Only if they're third-class male," I said somberly. "First-class female is a whole different thing."

She played with it a while. "Well, you certainly *talk* like a detective," she said. "Are you?"

I nodded.

Her eyes flicked with doubt. "But you're gray," she said. "I sort of expected someone —"

"What?"

"More colorful, I guess. Like Garfield, I suppose."

"You want a movie star," I said, "you buy a ticket to the movies. You want a detective, you've come to the right place."

"I hope so," she said.

I smiled encouragement and led her through the cool pleasant gloom of the bookstore and into my small cluttered office in the back, the desk lamp filling it with warm mellow light. Hunnicker had left a stack of books on the armchair and she settled on top of them, examining the spines.

"These are mysteries," she said.

"All books are mysteries till you've finished the last page. If you mean they're detective stories — right. It's all he sells." I settled at my desk. "So you want to talk fiction or you want to talk fact?"

She hesitated prettily and glanced at one of her nails. "I don't know where to start."

"You can start with your name, your address and your problem."

"My name," she said, "is Sugary." She had the sense to blush. "And my address is 12B."

"You mean you live in the building?"

"The penthouse."

At that one, I pricked up my ears. After all, I'm in business and a girl in a penthouse can afford to pay the fee.

I suppose she read my mind, or maybe just my ears. "I better ask you right now what your fee is," she said, "because I haven't got a —"

"Half a pound of lox plus expenses."

"Lox?"

"Smoked salmon?"

"Oh," she said. "Well . . . I guess so. I mean if you can wait till next Sunday."

"Then I'll have to have a small can of tuna in advance."

"You're a tough one," she said.

I was hungry, that was all. But if people want to figure me as tough, it's okay, and besides, it's good for business. I swiveled in my chair. "Let's talk about your problem."

"Of course," she said, and then watched her nail again for a while. "It's hard to just blurt out your problems to a stranger. Can I ask you about yourself?"

I shrugged. "It's your tuna. You can ask whatever you like. I'm four," I said. "I've been a detective all my life. I was born in a precinct."

"Don't joke," she said demurely.

"I'm serious. I was. The detective squad adopted me. I stayed for a year and a half."

"And then quit?"

"I didn't like the bureaucracy," I said.

"Bureaucracy?"

"A word meaning 'too many bosses and very

stupid rules.' Anyway, I quit and went into my own business." I smiled at her flatly. "Meaning I'm the boss and my stupidity's my own."

She appeared to think it over, looking at me gravely out of angel-blue eyes. Then offered, in a sudden little burst: "We were robbed."

"When?"

"I don't know. We went away for the weekend. We left Friday night? Anyway, we got back tonight and it was gone."

I waited.

"The jade necklace," she announced. "It belongs to Mrs. Simms."

"Your family's name is Simms?"

"No, we're the Crandles. Mr. Crandle's a jeweler. He *made* it for Mrs. Simms. And the jade, Mr. Crandle said, was very old and rare. And then he said he was ruined." Sugary started to cry.

I looked away at the ceiling. "What else can you tell me?"

"The terrace door was open and some flowerpots were smashed."

"The pots on the terrace?"

She nodded. "Mr. Crandle said a *cat* burglar did it." She was *really* bawling now.

I said, "Sugary, do you know what a cat burglar is?"

She sniffed at me. "It's either a cat who's a burglar, or a burglar who steals cats."

"Wrong twice," I said. "A cat burglar is a human being who's almost as smart and athletic as a cat."

"That's impossible!" she said.

"Well . . . they come close. So the burglar, like a cat, could have leapt from another terrace, or dropped himself down from the roof."

"No!" she said. "Yes?"

"Uh-huh."

"Could you find him? Could you find him and get the necklace?"

I didn't want to lie to her. Cracking a burglary case is tougher than cracking a walnut with your teeth, so I simply said, "I'd like to have a look at your apartment."

"When?" she said.

"When do the Crandles go to bed?"

"On Sundays? About . . . ten."

"Then I'll see you at twenty after."

"It's a date," she said and suddenly bounded off the chair. She turned in the doorway. "Oh merciful heavens, I forgot to ask your name."

"Sam," I said flatly.

"It's a date, Sam," she said.

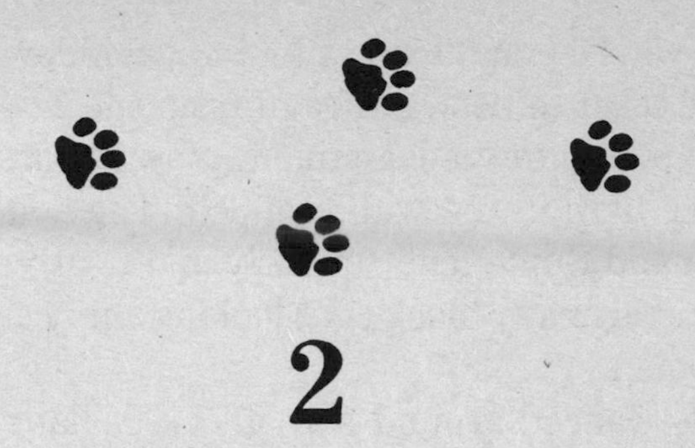

2

After Sugary had gone, I paced around the bookstore and kicked myself in the tail.

Of all the kinds of trouble I could possibly have bought myself, promising to look for a burglar was the worst.

Nobody ever finds burglars in New York and everybody knows it, especially burglars. In fact, we're so famous for not finding burglars that dangerous burglars from all around the world seem to come here for haven.

I settled at my desk. What I needed, I decided quickly, was a plan.

Either that, or a nap.

I was thinking it over when I heard a low familiar rumbling in the wall. It was the dumbwaiter coming. Personally, I'd define a dumbwaiter as a guy who spills the wrong kind of soup on your lap, but it's also the name for a funky little elevator — about the size of an oven and set in the wall where you'd expect to find a window. It used to be used to send garbage from the twenty-four apartments to the basement. Now it's used by us.

The hum in the wall stopped. The door sprung open and Spike leapt silently and neatly onto the desk, his heavy black coat looking shiny and newly groomed.

He glanced around the office. "What's up?" he said. "I thought I heard a soft purry voice."

Spike lives above me in apartment 2A.

"So you got yourself all spiffed up to take a look. Too late, kid, she's gone."

Spike sniffed the air. "*Who's* gone?" he said.

"The kitten in the penthouse." I swiveled in my chair.

"Sugary?"

I nodded. "You know her?"

"Not yet."

"You know anything about her?"

Spike cocked his head. His roommate's a city-side reporter for the *Post* and Spike likes to see himself as carrying forward the traditions of the press. In other words, he's nosy.

On the other hand, he's good.

"Well . . . put it this way," he admitted. "Not enough. Not as much as I'd like to. They only moved in about four, five weeks ago."

"Memorial Day weekend," I said. "To be exact."

Spike looked offended. "If you know, why ask?"

"What I *don't* know," I said, "is thing one about the Crandles."

"Good. I never did like a know-it-all, you know."

"I know," I said dryly.

Spike rolled his eyes. "There are two of them," he said. "The woman works at an office, the man works at home. It also appears they go away every weekend."

"So," I said. "Everybody knows they go away."

"Not *every*body."

"Yeah? Just you and who else?"

"And Sue."

"And if Sue knows, everybody knows." Sue's the night manager of Kitten Kaboodle, the shop next door to me — a combination beauty parlor/boarding house/boutique.

"I suppose," Spike conceded. "What difference does it make? So they're gone every weekend and everybody knows. So what?"

"So their apartment was robbed this weekend."

"Aha." Spike stared at me and thoughtfully scratched his ear. "And she came here to . . . what? To cry on your shoulder?"

"Relax," I said. "She came here to put me on the case."

Spike grinned. "When do we start?"

"We?" I said.

"Listen — for a case this impossible, you'll surely need an assistant."

I stared at him steadily. "Right," I said poker faced. "In fact — starting now. I want to check with the street cats."

"The *street*?" he said, outraged. "Now? In this heat?"

"And then, at ten-twenty, I'm meeting her up at the penthouse."

"Right." Spike nodded. "I'll see you at ten o'clock."

The alley was as airless as the inside of a cow. At the edge of it, a bright, almost gaudy full moon tried to creep over a rooftop. It wasn't trying hard. It ran out of energy halfway over the water tank and hovered there in a crouch.

There's a nook in the alley. It's filled with rotting furniture, a long row of garbage pails and cast-off appliances. Butch, on a banged-up blue velvet love seat with its stuffing coming out, was talking quietly with Jane. Jane sat gnawing on its blue velvet arm.

"Nice night," she said sullenly. "What brings you out?"

"Do I have to have a reason?"

"Tonight you do," she said. "It's a hundred-and-twelve degrees."

She was wet and gummy and smelled of sardines, but I smiled at her anyway. "I came to shoot the breeze."

"*What* breeze?" Butch looked at me. "There hasn't been a breeze here since 1982." He scratched at his shoulder blade, stirring up mosquitoes in his flat yellow fur. "You all revved up, man. Look like you got a little business on your mind."

"A little," I said.

"How little?"

"Little milk and a three-ounce can of Friskies. I could leave it on the windowsill."

"Yeah? Trade for what?"

"For whatever you know about a recent B and E. Cat-burglar style."

"B and E? Spells 'be.' " Jane shifted in her seat.

"B and E meaning Breaking and Entering," Butch explained. And to me: "Where'd it happen — this alleged B and E?"

"On a ledge," I said dryly. "At apartment 12B."

"Faces Tenth Street, huh?"

I nodded.

"Then you better check Angie up at Tenth. She's been there from about Wednesday. Last time I saw her she was sleeping over a stoop."

"Who's Angie?"

"Angora. Tan-colored. Tough. You go to see Angie, man, you better sharpen your nails."

Tenth Street is angled off the left side of the

alley. It's a street lined with brownstones — five-story houses that were built of brown stone. Originally, I guess, in the 1800s, they were one-family houses. Now they're apartments, but they still have a restful kind of old-fashioned charm. Little front porches. Big bay windows. Window boxes studded with geraniums and greens.

The street was deserted. The only thing going was the air-conditioning units, exhaling their hot clammy breath on the street. I checked out the first two buildings on the left. Silent. Empty. The third had a stoop — a short stone staircase that led to a front porch. There were boxes in the windows but there weren't any flowers. A matted Angora was sprawled in the first box.

"Angie?"

She glowered.

"Can I talk to you for a minute?" I leapt to the windowsill. She arched for a fight. "Just talk," I said defensively.

"Sure. That's what they all say. Why don't you go away and talk to somebody else?"

"Because I think you can help me. I'm investigating a robbery," I said. "Across the street."

"You a cop?" she said.

"Private. Did you see something?"

Silence. She shrugged and looked away. "Okay, so what if I did? It's just people, man. Who cares what people do to each other, huh?"

"C'mon, Angie. Gimme a break."

She shrugged. "In which leg?"

I laughed.

"I wasn't kidding."

"Didn't think you were," I said. "But let's try another angle. There's a lady I know puts food out every morning. Help me on this one, I'll give you her address."

She measured me carefully and then looked away. "Okay," she said finally. "What do you want to know?"

"What you saw. And when."

"You said *one* robbery? I saw three. Middle of Saturday night."

"Cat burglar?"

"Right. Guy lowered himself from the roof. Went straight to the penthouse. Went in, came out. Then he threw a rope down and lowered himself to the eighth. Same story. In and out. Then he leapt to another terrace. Oh man, it was like a movie."

I looked at her flatly. "And you had a box seat. — Okay. Final round: Can you describe the guy?"

"Nope. Only thing I saw, he was dressed all in black. Now it's *your* turn." She glared at me with pale slitted eyes. "Unless you're one of those guys that's all talk and no food."

"127 East 9th Street," I said.

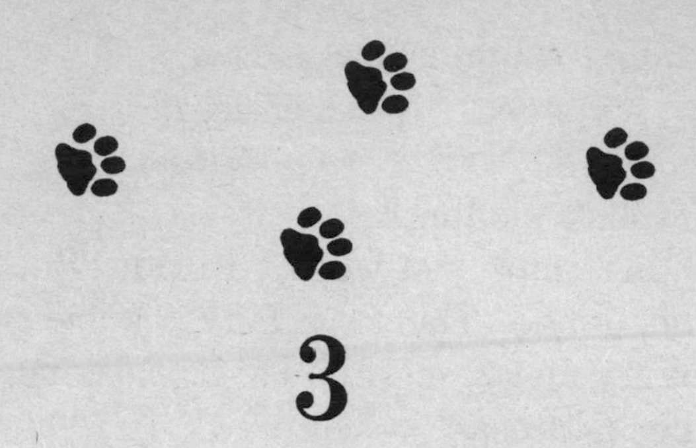

3

Sugary was pacing. "You're late," she said. "And early. The police haven't come and the Crandles are still awake."

Spike and I leapt from the elevator to the floor. It was 10:27. From where we were standing, in the darkness of the kitchen, I could hear the faint burbling of a television commercial and see a faint spattering of dust-moted light.

"They're in the living room," she said and looked quizzically over at Spike, who elbowed me in the ribs.

"Sugary," I said, catching on, "this is Spike."

Sugary merely nodded. Spike was left standing with an overanxious smile and a half-extended paw as the kitten looked at the clock. "It's 10:28," she said. "What do we do now?"

I suggested that we all stop looking at the clock and take a look at the scene of the crime.

"The workshop?" she said.

"Wherever the necklace was."

"The workshop," she said.

We followed her through the kitchen — Sugary's nails going *click-click-click* against the gloss of linoleum — and out to a carpeted floor.

It belonged to a dining room: table, four chairs, and a glass-doored cabinet with three narrow shelves. There were candlesticks in it and a couple of platters and a big shiny bowl.

"Silver," I said to Spike.

"Silver*plate*," he said. "Tin."

I glanced at a painting that was hung at the side of the door.

"A Picasso," I observed.

"A reproduction," Spike announced.

Sugary cocked her head. "Are you snobs?" she said. "Or what?"

"We're detectives," I told her.

"Oh," she said thoughtfully. "Well . . . here we are."

Where we were was in the workshop. It was part of the dining room. The room was divided by a floor-to-ceiling cabinet with several dozen drawers. Only one drawer was open. Near it, against the wall and underneath the window, was a felt-covered table and a striped canvas chair.

On the chair was a postcard addressed to the Crandles: "*Dear Jack and Marie . . .* "

"Is that a clue?" Sugary said.

I ignored her entirely and looked at the cabinet — the one open drawer. "Did Mr. Crandle touch the drawers? Or is this the way you found it?"

"The way we found it," Sugary said. "Mr. Crandle said we shouldn't touch anything at all until we talk to the police." She cocked her pretty head. "Is that a clue?" she said.

"Yes."

I looked around the room again and followed my own thought:

The cat burglar seemed to know exactly where to go. To exactly which drawer. He hadn't taken the candlesticks, the platters or the bowl. Because he knew they weren't silver? Or because he only wanted jade.

Standing there thinking, I was suddenly distracted by something I merely felt. Sensed, is more the word. The room had an undertaste — an odor I couldn't place. But whatever it was, it was only in the workshop and not in the rest of the room.

I turned back to Spike. "Take a breath," I said carefully, "and tell me what you smell."

He sniffed, sniffed again. "I smell something I've never smelled."

"Can you smell it in the dining room?"

Spike went to check. Now Sugary took a sniff.

"Is that familiar to you?" I said.

First she shook her head. “It’s nothing Mr. Crandle ever uses in his work. And it *cer*tainly isn’t food.” She took another breath. “But I think I’ve smelled it before.”

“Where?” I said. “When?”

Frowning, deep in thought, she seemed to focus on the air. “This is hard,” she said. “The smell is so faint it’s hardly there. I mean, if you hadn’t mentioned it —”

Spike cut her off. “Not in the dining room, not in the kitchen. Now what?” he said.

“Now we go to the terrace.”

Sugary said we couldn’t. The only way to the terrace was to go through the living room, and the Crandles were in the living room. “And not only that, it’s got a major white carpet and we wouldn’t exactly blend.”

“There’s another way,” I said, and moved to the felt table and up to the open window.

Another quick move and I was standing on the ledge.

If you’d call it a ledge.

It wasn’t much wider than the shadow of a snail. My feet had to stand on a line, single file.

Did that stop me? Not me. If I’d had any brains I’d be teaching mathematics instead of chasing thieves, so I didn’t even flinch.

I stood on the window ledge and gazed at the night.

Out there below me was a hot toy city with dark toy secrets. Small men and women, the size of tin soldiers, paraded down the street. Cars, like caterpillars, slept beneath the trees.

This was scary but fun. A prickle of excitement exploded in my head and then spread through my body. It was great to be alive. I hunkered back for leverage and looked at the terrace rail — a strip of wrought iron at the other side of the world, about five feet away. And then I was airborne — defier of gravity — my muscles taut, my body stretched to its limits, my fast blood pulsing with the ecstacy of flight. I landed gently and closed my eyes with a grin. Eagle. King of the hill.

"Ready or not," Spike yelled at me suddenly, "here . . . I . . . come!"

He whooped like Tarzan and jetted into the air.

"Ka-*boom*," he said as he landed, then called back to Sugary, "ready, set, go!"

Sugary didn't move. She sat on the window, half in, half out, looking fearfully down at the street.

"I . . . I've never been on a ledge before," she said, and her voice really quivered. "I don't think I can do it."

"Of course you can do it," I told her. "You're a cat."

"I'm a *house* cat!" she wailed, "and I'm also not

a fool. You know, a lot of cats *die* from taking leaps out of windows and I'll tell you something else. That line about a cat's always landing on her feet? Forget it, Sam. I leapt from the refrigerator once and you know where I landed? I landed on my —"

"Sugary!" I snapped. "This isn't a refrigerator."

"*You're* telling *me!*"

"It's an emergency!" I said.

At least it made her move. She gave it another beat and then slowly, uncertainly, lifted her feet to the ledge and then stood, tense and shivering and staring down at the street.

"Hey!" I said. "Don't look down. Look at me."

She lifted her eyes again. "Sam . . . ?"

"Just do it!"

It didn't take her long. She took a deep breath and then rose off her legs, arcing gracefully like a dancer. For a moment she was just a blonde blur in the air. Then she was standing, looking dazed, next to Spike.

"You're a natural," I said.

She offered me a smile of such deep glowing joy, if I remembered it slowly it could last me till Christmas. "I *loved* it," she said.

"Uh-huh. Let's go to work."

The sliding glass door to the living room was open. The television flickered its pale beam of light onto overturned flowerpots and shards of terra cotta and the night's single victim — a clump of chrysanthemums, withering in the heat.

I examined the edge of the door. It was framed in aluminum and set on aluminum tracks. No scratches. No dents. No evidence of tampering. Interesting, I thought. So the burglar didn't pick any locks; he had a key.

And there was that smell again, faint but distinctive. The scent of the burglar? I had to check it out.

I looked at the Crandles, sitting stunned on a dark green corduroy sofa — a redheaded woman with a tight, sad expression on a round pleasant face, the dark-haired man staring absently at the movie and chewing the edge of his nail.

I looked at the white carpet.

I looked at the glass lamp.

I looked up at Spike. "That table in the corner. Would you say it's simply old or would you say it's antique?"

"I'd say . . ." he said, squinting, "I'd say . . . it's very possibly a genuine Sheraton. Eighteen thirty or perhaps 'thirty-one."

"Sugary?" I nodded. "Go jump on that table."

"Not *that* one," she said. "Oh I couldn't. It's not allowed."

"I know it's not," I said. "Which is why I want

you to do it. It's called a diversion. You divert their attention while I get into the room."

"Alone?" Spike said.

"Right. Your assignment is to check the rest of the house."

"Check for what?"

"For that smell."

Spike turned around and leapt silently back to the window.

"Sugary? You're on again. Ready, set, go."

Everything happened at once. Sugary was on the table, the Crandles were on their feet — a lot of "Sugary! Get off there!" — and I was into the room.

I did what I had to do and ended up in the workshop.

Spike trotted in. "Nope," he said. "Nothing. I didn't smell a thing except peanut butter, socks, and Calvin Klein's Obsession."

"Right," I said. "Figures."

"*What* figures?" Sugary slunk into the room. She glowered in my direction. "Boy, I hope it was worth it. I've never *been* so embarrassed."

"It was worth it." I grinned at her. "Here's what we've learned. The burglar had a key. He let himself in and went straight to the workshop — di*rec*tly to the workshop. His smell's on the carpet just as plain as an arrow."

"So?" she said.

"So — he knew exactly what he wanted and exactly where it was."

"Meaning?"

"I don't know, except he's been here before."

"Before?" Sugary said.

And before I could explain it, the doorbell was ringing, the Crandles were at the door, and a couple of policemen were standing in the hall.

4

They entered the room the way cops enter rooms, walking heavily in their shoes. The equipment at their belts — an assortment of handcuffs, radios and weapons — made a harsh half-musical military sound: jingling of metal, crackling of static, creaking of leather.

One of them was huge — a big, broad man with a belly like a pillow, and a thatch of gray hair. His partner was a rookie — a new-at-the-job cop — very young, very slim. His name tag pegged him as "W. Hernandez." The guy with the belly was "R.A. McFee," and appeared to be a sergeant.

"Sorry to keep you waiting," the sergeant said abruptly, "but we made some other stops." He paused dramatically. "So did your burglar."

Sugary looked at me. "Eighth floor," I whispered. "The Kellys and the Cohens."

"Eighth floor," McFee said. "The Kellys and the Cohens."

Spike said, "They also go away every weekend."

I nodded. "I know," and looked over at Hernandez who was crouched near the terrace and checking the edge of the door.

At this point, the three of us were listening intently from a hiding place in the hall. The Crandles, on the couch, were beyond my line of vision. What I saw was Hernandez and a half of McFee who was sitting on a straight-backed green-and-white chair. Or, at any rate, the center of his body was sitting. The rest of his bulk seemed suspended in the air.

He'd begun to ask questions. He asked what was stolen then appeared to be surprised. "Just the necklace? No cash? No silver? No gold?"

"Just the necklace," Crandle said, and then began to describe it. The jade, he said, was twenty individual pieces of a pale perfect green that were shaped into leaves. What made them so priceless wasn't only the astounding perfection of the stones and the skill of whoever had originally carved them, but the fact that they were nearly twelve hundred years old.

McFee wrote it down. "Then they're insured," he said. "Right?"

Crandle said flatly, "And so's the Mona Lisa."

McFee raised his eyes.

"Listen. The money's not the point here, officer. We're talking about art. We're talking about history. Imagine it. Imagine holding something in your hand that was held by another man twelve hundred years ago."

McFee didn't get it; but the way Crandle told it put a shiver up my spine. I started picturing a guy in some Chinese village in the year 800 carving leaves out of stone.

Pictures like that are what I like about people. I liked Jack Crandle. I liked the way he cared. I wanted to help him find the jade and keep his job.

Hernandez, coming back from the terrace, interrupted. "Like the other two," he said. "Door to the terrace wasn't busted here either."

"Meaning," McFee said, "your burglar had a key."

"To the terrace?" Jack Crandle didn't like the explanation. "That's impossible, Sergeant. Nobody's got the —"

"No. Not the key to the terrace, sir. The key to the front door."

Spike made a low, pained gurgle in his throat.

McFee blathered on: "You see, the terrace wasn't used as an entry point at all."

"But they're wrong," Sugary said. "Aren't they?"

I nodded. Then I looked at Hernandez.

"It's obvious," he said.

"Well now, it's obvious to *us*," McFee added. "After all, we're detectives."

Spike rolled his eyes.

Sugary looked doubtful. "Sam . . . ?" she said.

"*Ssh.*"

I listened as McFee-the-detective spelled it out. The way he had it figured, the burglar got in with a key to the front door. Then he opened the terrace door, kicked over the flowerpot, and tried to make it *look* as though he'd come from the terrace.

But he couldn't fool a red-hot cop like McFee. No sir. No way.

"So the question now," McFee said, "is who's got your key? Or, let me put it this way: There's a handyman in the building. Guy's got the key to both the Kellys' and the Cohens'. Guy's name is . . . what's the guy's name?" he asked Hernandez.

"Max," Hernandez said.

"*Max??*" Spike was horrified. "The cops suspect *Max*?"

"Not *Max*," Sugary said.

"Max," McFee repeated. "So did Max have your key?"

Mrs. Crandle said reluctantly, "Well . . . yes, he does. But I wouldn't —"

"Second question: Has he been here alone?"

"Well . . . yes," she said. "He's come to feed Sugary once or twice —"

"Seven times," Sugary said.

"And then he supervised the painting."

McFee looked around and checked the pictures on the wall. "Which one?" he said.

"No, not the painting. The *painting*." Jack Crandle sounded angry. "When the apartment was painted, he was —"

"Oh," McFee said. "When was that?"

"Back in June."

"And was the necklace here?"

"Yes."

"And the plumbers," Mrs. Crandle said. "He supervised the plumbers."

"When was that?"

"July third."

"Okay, there you have it." McFee made some notes. "Your handyman, Max, had some time to look around. And whoever your thief was, he knew what he wanted and exactly where it was." He nodded, then rose. "Same thing happened in the other two apartments. He seemed to know the jewelry was hidden in the freezer and the cash was in a shoe."

I motioned to Sugary. The cops and the Crandles started heading for the door and we moved to another wall.

"Are you sure?" Marie Crandle wasn't happy with the news.

"As sure as we can get without the proof," Hernandez said.

"And we'll get it. Wait and see." McFee closed his notebook and opened the front door.

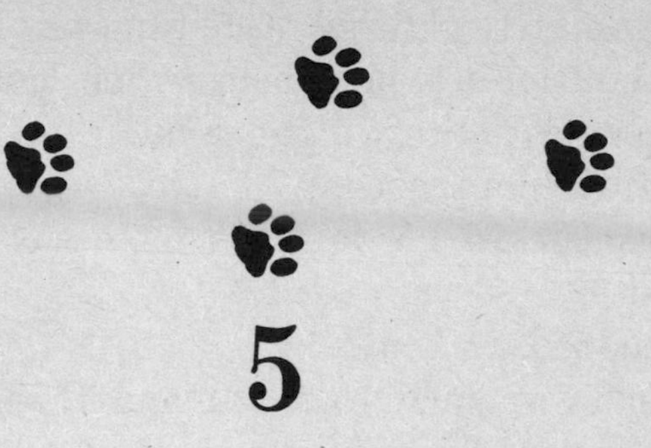

5

Sugary looked at me and slowly shook her head. "Oh Sam," she said. "Listen. It absolutely positively couldn't've been Max."

We were back in the bookstore. Sugary was sitting on the books on the chair. Spike and I were eating from a still-warm carton of sweet-and-sour pork that the Crandles had ordered, eaten little of, and left.

"It just couldn't." She looked at me quizzically. "Could it?"

"Not unless he came from the terrace, wearing black. I've got a witness, remember? Besides," I said, chewing on a Chinese vegetable I couldn't identify, "it's not in his character."

Spike said, "He's one of the finer human beings. Considerate, thoughtful —"

"And gentle," Sugary said. "And fun," she added quickly. "Like he'd come to do dinner? So he'd never just toss a can of glop on the floor, he'd always stop to play ball. One time we played hide-and-seek for a whole hour." She looked at me bleakly. "What're we gonna do?"

"Prove him innocent," I said.

Spike licked his lips. "A lot easier said than done."

I nodded. "I know."

Sugary seemed to moan and then hung her head dejectedly over the edge of a book. "This is terrible," she said in a sad defeated voice. "This is just the worst night of my whole entire life."

I looked at her flatly. "All seventeen months of it."

"Hey listen, Sam. Don't talk down to me," she said. "Maybe I'm young, but I know how to suffer."

"We're all suffering," Spike said. "Sam is, too. He just doesn't like to show it."

I said nothing and finished eating.

I pushed away the carton. It was ten after midnight. It was time to get to work.

The Kit-Kat Klub is one of those dives on the edge of the East Village. A dive is something like a nightclub, only lower, which is why it's called a dive.

The entrance to the Kit-Kat was rundown and

dirty. A blue neon sign, only half of it working, blinked IT AT UB.

The neighborhood was foul. A deserted warehouse with its windows busted out stood yawning like an old toothless giant in the dark. The rest of the street held abandoned tenements and long-empty lots.

I looked at the club again. IT AT UB. A sweaty-looking bouncer leaned flat against the door. I once defined a bouncer as a two-way doorman. He's the guy who lets you in and the guy who kicks you out.

I wasn't sure he'd let me in.

And then I got lucky. The door swung open. A waiter came out with a sandwich and a Coke, which he handed to the bouncer while I beat it through the door.

Inside, it was blue. Everything was blue. The carpet, the ceiling, the furniture, the mood. Jazz floated over thick smoky air. Not loud hard rock; this was soft dreamy jazz. People dressed in everything from sequins to jeans filled the small round tables. A couple of musicians blew music from the stage.

I squinted through the bad-smelling, eye-stinging air till I found the guy I wanted. Tom hadn't changed. His tail was still bushy and his eyes were still bright.

I motioned. He waved, made a big happy grin, and came trotting across the floor.

"Long time," he said. "Man. Haven't seen you since . . . when?"

"Since the Jackson case," I said.

"That's the one," he said, nodding. "The 7-95."

I laughed. Tom and I had been roommates at the precinct, and he still knew the codes. A 7-95 is a missing person.

"What's it this time?" he said.

"An 11-26."

"A burglary? Hey. Lotsa luck," he said dryly.

"Is Scratch around?"

"Yeah. Back office. He's been cozied up with Cheater for an hour."

"Cheater still in business?"

"Hey," Tom looked at me. "Is water still wet?"

"Right." I said.

Cheater Rivera is a fence. A fence is a guy who buys stuff that's been stolen, from the burglars who stole it. Cheater's specialty is hot stolen jewels. Scratch is his roommate.

Tom said, "You want to see Scratch, you'll have to wait. Door to that office's locked tighter'n a tomb."

I sat in a shadow and listened to the sweet blue harmonies of jazz. Once in a while the clarinetist hit a note that made my neck hairs ripple, and I thought about Max.

Talk about the blues, Max was in much deeper trouble than he knew.

I turned at the sudden sound of voices in the hall.

"Nice going," Cheater said, his voice leaking out at me from underneath the door. "It's a pleasure doing business."

The door clicked open.

"Yeah. And the pleasure's all yours," a man said. He turned in the doorway — a balding burglar wearing rundown Reeboks and a dirty pair of sweats.

Cheater, in a cream-colored suit, cracked a grin. "Like your mama done told you, kid. Crime doesn't pay." He laughed and checked his watch.

I peered into the office. Scratch, on a table, sat slurping a plate of cream.

"I got a meeting," Cheater said. "C'mon, kid. I'll walk you." He fumbled at the wall switch and slapped off the light.

Under cover of darkness, I streaked through the door.

The door locked behind me. *Click-click-click.*

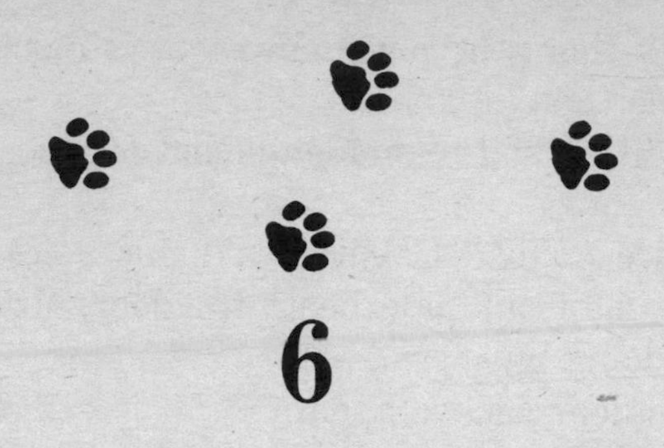

6

My eyes adjusted to the darkness of the room and I checked it out fast.

Dark heavy curtains were drawn across the window. A desk in the corner held a laptop computer and a push-button phone. Behind it, on the wall, was a huge oil painting that I knew hid the safe.

Scratch, still lapping at his cream, hadn't moved, hadn't lifted his eyes. He was pure dead white. His fur was the color of an undercooked fish, and he looked as though he'd gained about two thousand pounds. The ultimate fat cat. A monument to greed.

"Well-well-well," he said, without looking up. "I figured you'd show your face sooner or later." He wiped at his whiskers with a stuffed-looking paw. "I just hoped it would be later."

I shrugged. "How it goes."

"Speaking of going," Scratch said, "why don't you?"

I jumped on the table and looked him in the eye. "Listen, my fine furry friend," I said darkly. "You owe me one, remember?"

He pushed away the cream dish and started on a leftover hot pastrami sandwich, getting mustard on his chin. Buried in the wide fleshy furrows of his neck was a diamond-studded collar.

"So," he said, eating, "how's the honesty business?"

"Try it," I said. "It's like a thirty-day diet."

He laughed and looked up. "Good shot," he said levelly. "You're still lean and mean. — Okay. What's your pitch?"

I explained about the jade and my hunt to retrieve it. "So I want to know if anybody brought it here," I said.

"Twenty leaves." Scratch nodded. "Hanging on a new but very classy gold vine. No clasp," he said. "It looked like the jeweler wasn't finished."

"Have you got it here?"

"Sorry, kid. The Cheater wouldn't buy it. He told the guy the stuff was too old and too rare. He said an item like that, there'd be cops all over it." Scratch flicked his head in the direction of the safe. "He took some other stuff, though."

"You mean," I said carefully, "a pair of diamond

earrings, a diamond engagement ring, and two diamond pins."

"And I won't even ask you," Scratch said, "how you know."

I knew because I'd seen Mrs. Jane Kelly's jewels, and the Kellys — in apartment 8A — had been robbed.

I thought for a second.

If I couldn't help the Crandles then maybe, just maybe, I could still help the Kellys.

I leapt very neatly from the table to the desk. The big oil painting that covered up the safe was like a shutter on a hinge.

I batted it open and squinted at the safe.

Scratch said, "Forget it. First of all, I don't even know the combination."

"But you know Cheater's birthday."

He grinned. "April third."

"What year?"

He made a shrug.

Okay, I thought. Cheater looked to be about thirty. So I did some arithmetic. A person who was thirty in 1993 . . . ninety-three minus thirty . . . He'd been born in sixty-three.

April third, sixty-three.

People with safes that have combination locks use their birthdays as the codes. At least, frequently they do, so I figured, worth a try.

I stood with my two front paws against the wall.

Then I lifted my right one and fiddled with the dial.

April, I thought. It's the one, two, three . . . fourth month of the year.

I spun the dial to the left till it landed on the "4" and made a satisfying click. So far, I was right. Then I spun it around again and made it hit the "3."

Good. Another click.

Then another quick spin and I hit the "63."

Nothing.

No clicking sound to tell me I was right.

I stopped, thought again.

It took another three guesses, but Cheater, it appeared, was thirty-seven years old.

The safe popped open and yawned at me. Empty.

Behind me, Scratch laughed.

"I could've told you that," he said. "Cheater walked out with all the stuff in his pocket."

"Nice," I said.

"And nice to see you still know your stuff. So we're even," Scratch said. "I owed you one, buddy, and I told you Cheater's birthday and that's all you get."

I grabbed him by the collar. I pulled very tight. "Want to talk about even, I could pull even harder."

He looked at me defiantly: "Pull even harder."

I pulled even harder.

"Okay," he said. *"Stop!"*

"First," I said, "tell me who's the guy that brought the jade."

"His name? I don't know. Will you lighten up a little?"

I lightened up. A little. "Then tell me what he looks like."

"You saw him. Just now."

I let go of Scratch's collar and I heard myself groan.

So the bald guy in sweats had been Jack Crandle's burglar and I'd watched him walk away. With the jade in his pocket.

I glanced at the door. Cheater had locked it with a *click-click-click*. Or as Tom put it ominously, "tighter'n a tomb." I was locked in with Scratch, whom I'd irritated greatly, and I didn't have a plan.

Then suddenly I did. Because suddenly a loud clap of thunder hit the air. A breeze pushed the drapes. Well well, I thought rapidly. Somewhere behind them a window had been open.

I leapt to the windowsill.

Scratch sat glowering and rubbing his fat neck.

7

I want to get it straight that I'm no fan of violence. People who go around punching other people are as dumb as baboons. There are only two exceptions that I learned at the precinct. Two situations when a decent man fights.

One: in self-defense or in defense of someone else, and two: in defense of some moral idea. That's it and that's all. Everything else is baboon behavior.

I figured I was out for some moral idea when I was grappling with Scratch, but I didn't like to do it.

I looked at the sky. The rain coming down was like a thick beaded curtain. A shower curtain. Right. And boy, was I wet. I glanced at my sodden reflection in a puddle. I looked like a seal.

When I'd jumped from the window, I'd felt myself landing on a rubble-filled lot. An obstacle course full of old rusty metal and jagged tin cans that were hungry for my feet. But I'd picked my way out of it and got to the sidewalk and now I was safe.

The street was deserted.

A sharp bolt of lightning cut through the air like a zigzagging zipper unzipping the night.

I stood for a moment at the edge of the warehouse and thought about possibly using it for shelter. Jump through the fragments of the busted-out window, lie low, wait it out. But the glass was too spiky. It rose from the window like the teeth of a dark shark.

It must have been the next loud trumpeting of thunder that hid the other sound — the sound of disaster that was barking at my heels.

I turned.

He was big. A broad-bodied schnauzer with murder in his eyes.

My back went up. I stood there frozen, not certain what to do. If I ran, I'd be chicken. If I stayed, I'd be meat. Besides, if I ran I'd be asking him to chase me.

I waited.

He pounced.

He was big but he was slow.

By the time he got near me, I was six feet away.

I'd jumped to the ledge of that cat-eating window and I hung there and growled.

He didn't seem to care.

He stood there barking and jumping at the wall, and I knew from experience he'd stay there forever. We'd both die of hunger before he went away.

The next move was mine. It was something I'd seen in an old-fashioned movie. A cowboy jumping from the edge of a rooftop and landing on his horse.

I landed — bull's-eye — right on his back. He didn't know what had hit him but he couldn't get it off.

He tried to turn his head around and bite me. He couldn't.

He rolled; I rolled with him.

He growled; so did I.

He bucked; I dug my nails in.

He tried to run away which was not a brilliant plan since I was riding on his back and he couldn't outrun me.

Still, he kept trying. The more he couldn't lose me, the faster he ran.

Up to First Avenue. Over to Tenth Street.

He kept on running while the rain kept falling and the sky kept erupting with the thunder and the light. Once in a while, he'd look over his shoulder, see me, get spooked, and try an extra burst of speed.

When we got to Eighth Avenue, I jumped off his back, but he didn't seem to notice. He just kept running.

I stood for a moment in the shelter of an awning. I felt like a jockey who's just won the Derby. Or a rare, lucky man who's caught a taxi in the rain.

The rain seemed to lighten, then tapered to a stop.

I walked home singing.

8

Sue was still awake. She was sitting in the window of Kitten Kaboodle. As she saw me approaching it, she tapped on the glass, then motioned to me, frowning.

I stopped, cocked my head. I was sodden and chilled and the thought of her company was comforting and warm.

I jumped through her mail slot and landed on the floor in a wet sliding skid.

"Good *grief*," she said. "What were you doing on the streets?"

For an answer, I sneezed.

That's all she had to hear. Two minutes later I was sitting on one of her beauty parlor chairs with the nozzle of a hairdryer pointing at my flanks.

Its humming made it much too difficult to talk but she communicated nicely with a loud, ringing glare. Sue can glare louder than anyone I know.

She's a green-eyed redhead — high-tailed, long-limbed, short-haired and sassy.

The dryer clicked off and her mouth clicked on.

"Hotshot detective. Macho man," she said. "Hasn't got the sense to come in out of the rain." She paused and cocked her head. "Or possibly you couldn't detect it was raining."

"It was raining," I was forced to concede, "cats and dogs."

"I have never understood that expression," Sue sniffed. "And I don't think I want to."

I explained about the dog.

She tried to keep an attitude of stony disapproval but she broke down and giggled.

"*Rode* him?" she said.

I nodded.

She was fixing me a warm dish of milk. She'd learned how to operate the microwave oven and took a lot of unexpected pride in her cooking.

By now we were sitting on a counter in the back — the door to the guest rooms behind us on the left, a pink quilted sofa beside us on the right, and a fair breeze blowing through the pink flowered drapes.

"Tell me more," she said, shoving me the warm plate of milk. "Tell me about the case."

I told her about the case. I liked the way she listened — all eyes, all ears.

"Sugary," she said, "is awfully sweet, don't you think?" She'd put the accent on "awfully."

I looked at her and grinned. I said, "Stop being catty."

"Who me?" she said. "Never."

I smiled and sipped milk.

"On the other hand," she said, "it's truly awful about Max. It's so completely unfair. And I bet when old Meany hears . . . *pschew*!" She made a sound like a gun being fired.

I winced. She was right. Meany — no kidding — is the guy who owns the building. Horton F. Meany. I couldn't make it up. And the man fits the name. And if Meany found out about Max — that he was even sus*pec*ted of a crime — *pschew*! It was definite that Max'd be fired.

I was silent for a time.

"Sam? You all right?"

"Yeah. Just thinking."

"Think aloud," she said. "Otherwise I tend to get lonely."

"I think," I said, "the burglar had the key to the terrace door. To all three terrace doors. So how'd he get the key?"

"Are you asking?"

"I'm thinking."

"You think," she said, "he'd been to the Crandles' place before. And he also must have been to the Kellys' and the Cohens'."

I nodded. "So the question is: Who do they know in common?"

She shrugged at me. "Maybe it's the pizza man," she said. "Or the guy who delivers laundry."

"Not," I said. "I saw him."

"Oh," she said. "Right."

I thought for a minute and finished off the milk in a hard single gulp, the warm liquid fire of it trickling into my limbs. I said, "Tell me something, Red."

She said, "Don't call me Red."

I said, "Tell me something, Sue."

She said, "Better."

"Okay. So how about any other robberies on the block. Have you heard of any?"

"Nope." She licked the last drop of milk. "How about the neighborhood," she said. "Does that count?"

I looked at her. "Answer that question yourself."

She nodded. "It counts. Okay. There was Sandy. They were robbed July fourth. He told me about it Thursday while Harry did his nails. There was also Lady Anne. Poor dear. We had to give her that disgusting shampoo. She got *fleas*, if you can imagine." Sue grinned at me suddenly. "And you know where she got them?"

I nodded. "In her hair."

She laughed. "In Beverly Hills — is that a hoot?" she said, "or what."

I frowned. "Get to the point."

"They were robbed last Saturday."

"How do you know Saturday?"

"Because," she said patiently, "Lady Anne was there."

"Bingo," I said. "I want her full name and address. And Sandy's, while you're up."

"C'mon, Sam." She looked hard at me. "You know I'm not supposed to."

"Hey, Red," I said, grinning. "If you'd done what you're supposed to, you'd still be in a butcher shop in Muncie, Indiana."

"True," she said cheerfully, and opened the appointment book and read me off the facts.

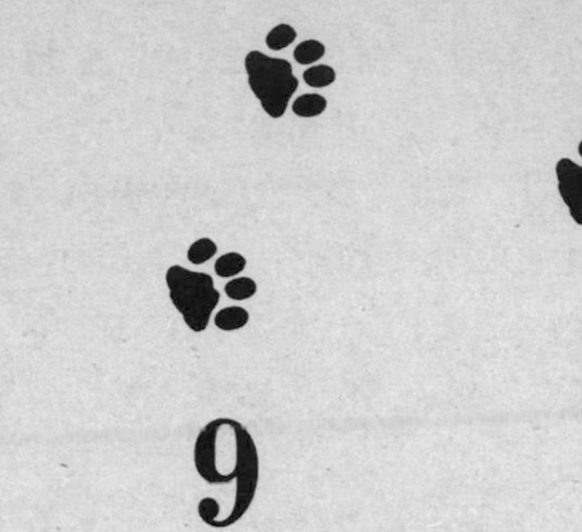

9

When I got to the bookstore, it was ten after four, the frayed end of the night. Even in a round-the-clock town like Manhattan, the discos and nightclubs are closed at four o'clock.

Meaning, the Kit-Kat Klub would be closed.

Meaning that Cheater and Scratch had gone home, and Tom, the night watchman, would be prowling on his own.

I moved to my desk, to the big square push-button, table-model phone. I batted the receiver neatly off the hook, pushed the button marked "Speaker," and punched out the number.

I listened to it ring, picturing the push-button phone in Cheater's office and hoping Tom could hear it.

While I waited, I booted up Hunnicker's computer and began a new file. I titled it *Jade*.

Tom must have answered on the seventeenth ring.

"Kit-Kat," he said.

"Can you do me a big favor?"

"Sam?" he said. "Sure."

"Okay. There's a laptop computer on the desk. Can you start it?"

A momentary silence, then, "Done."

"I was there at one o'clock and a bald guy was leaving. I figure he got there at . . . what? Twelve-thirty?"

"About," Tom said.

"So punch twelve-thirty and then today's date."

"So. You remember Cheater's codes," Tom said. "And today's July . . . twenty. Call it seven, two-oh."

The codework was simple. Cheater gave each of his clients a code name and kept them on file, and the file was cross-referenced. Meaning that every single item in the file, from the code name itself, to the jewelry he'd bought, to the times that he'd bought it, could be lifted from the file. And once you knew one of those facts, you'd get the others.

"Got it," Tom said. "Code name: Quark. Sold a diamond engagement ring —"

"I know," I said. "Skip it. When else was Quark there?"

"Last Sunday. That's the twelfth. Sold an emerald necklace and a Cartier watch. Also on the fifth. Quite a haul July fifth. He got twenty-three items. Want 'em all?"

"The two best."

"A thirty-carat diamond and a Patek Phillipe."

"What's a Patek Phillipe?"

"A watch," he said. "It's worth about 50,000 bucks."

"For a watch?" I said.

"People are crazy, man."

"Right."

"Moving on," he said dryly. He read off a total of four other dates.

I typed them all down. "Do me one other favor. If you see the guy —"

"Quark?"

"Yeah. Mr. Quark. If you see the guy —"

"You want me to follow him?"

"Right."

"You got it."

"Take care."

By the time I hung up I was almost too exhausted to make it up to bed. Bed is a soft brown corduroy pillow on a shelf near the ceiling. On the other hand, I figured if I settled on the floor, Hunnicker would wake me at the crack of ten o'clock.

So I climbed to the bookshelf and dropped off to sleep.

10

I woke in a lukewarm puddle of sunlight at twenty after one. The door between the office and the bookstore was open and Hunnicker was blathering to someone in the store. He'd left coffee on the desk and a half-eaten sandwich. It smelled like bacon and the double aromas sent me leaping out of bed.

There's a small bathroom that connects with the office. I did what almost everybody does in the morning, washed my face and paws, and stood squinting at the mirror, inspecting my whiskers.

Sue used to tell me I looked like I was wearing a gray flannel suit, open at the neck, with a white cotton shirt. She approved of the look. "Very corporate," she'd told me. "Very dressed for success."

I studied my reflection and tried to make a seriously gray flannel face — a face that could talk about sales charts and marketing and mortgages and golf.

I held it for a second till it cracked itself up. Then it grew serious all by itself. A dark fleeting shadow had passed across the glass.

I turned to the window. The bathroom mirror looks over at the window that overlooks the court. I jumped to the windowsill and hated what I saw:

Horton F. Meany moving quickly towards the street.

Two seconds later I was standing in the dumbwaiter, pressing on the "B," and a second after that, I was standing in the basement.

It was hot there and dark. At the end of the corridor, the laundry room was humming, and Oscar, a street cat, was watching the machines. Oscar thinks looking at a washing machine is like watching TV. His favorite entertainment, he says, is the soaps.

"Where's Max?" I said.

Oscar looked up at me and shrugged. "Butch asked me, too."

"Where's Butch?" I said.

"No. Where's Max?" Oscar said.

"*What?*" I said.

"Butch didn't ask me 'Where's Butch,' he asked me 'Where's Max.' "

"Oh," I said. "Right."

I turned from the laundry room and hurried

down the hall. Television junkies get water on the brain, and Oscar was the living waterlogged proof.

No Max in the office.

No Max in the hall.

One look at Meany and I'd thought about Max and what Sue had predicted. Or in other words: *pschew*!

I found myself desperately hoping I was wrong; then I felt hopeless.

Max was in the locker room, packing up his stuff.

I made a groan in my throat.

Max turned and looked at me. "Sam," he said softly. His broad face was worried. His eyes were full of shine — not exactly tears, but not exactly not. I leapt to the easy chair in front of the locker. Max put his big strong arm around my neck.

"Doh-sveeDANya," he said.

Max comes from Russia. He came to New York about six or seven years ago. It must have taken guts.

"Doh-sveeDANya" means good-bye.

"I be missink you," he whispered, and looked me in the eye. His eyes are very blue. Mine are very yellow, but our eyeballs, in any case, spoke the same language.

There's something I believe and you're free to think I'm nuts. But I've always thought the planet was divided into species. Not the physical species, like cats and dogs and horses and hens . . . I guess what I'm saying is that creatures are divided into species of the soul. And wherever you're going, you can find your own kin. Doesn't matter what their age or the color of their fur or the shape of their bodies or the number of their feet. A soul meets a soul and it knows if it's a brother and that's the end of that.

"Little brother," Max said. He sniffed, blew his nose in a clean yellow handkerchief, shoved it into his pocket, and zipped up the duffel bag that rested at his feet. On top of it, I noticed, was a nice framed picture of his wife and three kids.

I looked up and saw Butch. He was standing on the window ledge and peering through the screen. The glitter in his eyes was more angry than sad.

"Meany," Butch said. And the word said it all.

Max had his duffel bag slung from his shoulder. He'd picked up his jacket and was just about to go. Then he turned and saw Butch.

He put everything down again and walked to a cabinet and fished around the shelves. He came out with a large can of 9 Lives chicken in country gravy, opened it neatly, and placed it on a dish.

The last I saw of Max, he was feeding Butch and Jane.

11

Spike said, "I saw the whole story from the window. Cops . . . in and out. Meany . . . in and out. Max . . . out."

He was talking from his window. I was standing in the court, about twelve feet below. When I tried to look up at him, the sun was in my eyes.

"So now what?" he said.

"Now we get to work. Your assignment is to go up to Sugary's apartment."

"No hardship," he said, and began to lick his coat.

"No courtship, either. This is business, okay? Describe the bald burglar and —"

"*What* bald burglar?"

"Oh." I'd forgotten that I hadn't filled him in. I filled him in quickly. "Ask her if she's ever seen the guy before or if she knows who he is."

"And where are *you* going?"

"Out."

* * *

If I had the address right, Lady Anne Sternwood was living in a three-story mansion on Eleventh. I looked at the old brass numbers on the door, then jumped to the window ledge and checked my reflection in the spit-polished surface of the living room panes: Gray flannel suit, clean white shirt, white wool socks. I was everything the well-dressed detective ought to be. And about to introduce myself to twenty million bucks.

I jumped through the burglar-proof bars on the window and landed on the rug.

Inside, it was cool. Not air-conditioned cool. The room was like money that's been sitting in a vault. Untouched. Unwarmed by any hot little hands.

Thick white drapes had been drawn across the windows. Two white sofas stared blankly at each other, their cushions looking plumped and as rounded as geese.

The rug was Oriental.

The walls were a shiny and peculiar shade of red. A couple of tables seemed to wear the same color, and everywhere you looked there were huge flowered vases and shiny figurines.

"Dear heavens," said a deep-throated middle-aged voice, "I do hope you're not a burglar."

I turned. She was standing at the entrance from the hall. A pedigreed Persian, longhaired and plumpish and the color of ginger ale.

"Relax," I said politely. "I'm a private detective."

"Strange, I don't find that relaxing at all. In *fact* . . . I don't think I like private detectives much more than I like burglars. Who are you, young man?"

"I'm Sue's friend. Sam."

"Sue?" she said. "Oh. The little shopgirl at the shop."

"She's the manager," I said. "And she told me you were robbed. I came to ask a few questions."

"I see." She jumped languidly over to the sofa, not inviting me to sit. "And what were you expecting to collect for this service?"

"Answers," I said. "That was all I came to get."

"Mmm. How delightfully refreshing," she said, "in this age of greed and theft. If you'd like to sit down," she said, "not on the cushions, you can dangle from the arm."

I sat on the carpet.

"It's a Persian," she said.

"Beg pardon?"

"The carpet. The one we had before was just a little too French. The whole room, you see, was French. The year before, it was Spanish."

"The room," I said.

"Yes. Mrs. Sternwood redecorates every single year. Memorial Day weekend. Like clockwork, don't you see? And then they go away."

"For the summer?"

"But of course, my dear. The best people do."

"And they leave you here alone?"

For a quarter of a second, she looked a little sad. Then she lifted up her chin. "Not entirely alone. We've got a housekeeper, dear. Mrs. Clayton. Mrs. Clayton comes at least twice a week. And I've got my own amusements."

I looked around the room in which nothing, to me, looked tremendously amusing. No records, no books, no toys, no games.

Lady Anne had apparently caught my train of thought.

"I'm working on a needlepoint rug," she said defensively, and flashed her pretty nails. "I'm ripping out the flowers. First I ripped the yellow ones, now I'm on the reds. But enough about me, you want to talk about the thief."

I nodded. "First question: Can you tell me what he stole?"

"Of course I can, darling. An emerald necklace and a Cartier watch."

I smiled.

"Is that amusing?"

"No, but it fits."

According to Tom, Mr. Quark had sold exactly those items to Cheater. A week ago Sunday.

"And you saw the man," I said.

"It was terrifying. Yes. It was just after midnight —"

"Last Saturday."

"Yes. I was sleeping in the bedroom — up on the third floor? — and suddenly the door from the roof garden opened and there stood a man."

"Was he armed?"

"Well, of course he was *armed*, dear heart. He was also legged. Two arms, two legs."

"Uh-huh," I said deliberately. "How about guns?"

"No, he wasn't gunned. Nor do I believe he was batted or knifed. I can tell you he was clothed, and he was clothed all in black."

"Can you tell me what he looked like?"

"Sorry, dear," she said. "But they all look alike to me. Especially in the dark."

"And the door," I said, ignoring her comment, "was it locked?"

"It's always locked," she said. "What woke me was the faintest little click of the key. I'm a terribly light sleeper. Last summer I was awakened by a hiccough in New Jersey. Trenton, I believe."

"Uh-huh," I said. "Sort of like the princess and the pea."

"Ah, the princess." She nodded. "I know the lady well. And it wasn't a pea, dear. I think it was a pie. A large, quite uncomfortable huckleberry pie. Even peasants, I believe, would awaken from a pie."

"The burglar —" I said.

"All purple and squishy —"

"The burglar —" I said.

"All soggy and yick."

"The burglar," I reminded her. "He walked in and . . . what?"

"Oh," she said. "Him. He went directly to the hatbox."

"The jewels were in the box?"

"They were underneath the hat."

"One other question." I was eager to get away. "When the guy was in the bedroom, did you smell something funny?"

"*Smell?*" she said. "You think I got close enough to smell? I was hiding under a pillow. When he got to the hatbox, I ran to the other room."

"Good choice," I said, rising.

She walked me to the window.

"By the way," I said, turning for a moment on the ledge. "Did you enjoy Beverly Hills?"

"That was months ago," she said. "But I wouldn't recommend it. If you want my opinion —" She lowered her voice —"It's a town full of bloodsuckers, parasites and vermin."

"Fleas," I said thoughtfully.

"Fleas," she said. "Yes."

12

I left Lady Anne's having learned very little but confirming what I'd guessed. It's always important to confirm what you've guessed — to check it out, prove it, and tie it in a knot. The most important lesson I'd learned at the precinct was the one simple motto: Never Assume.

In fact, I decided, what I'd learned at Lady Anne's made the puzzle even harder.

Quark had very obviously been there before: 1) To get the key (or to make his own duplicate) and 2) to look around (and to learn that the jewelry was sitting in a hat).

So now I had a man who had previously visited the Crandles, the Kellys, the Sternwoods and the Cohens.

I hurried to the bookstore, hoping that Sugary could shed a little light.

As I walked across the courtyard, Spike, from

his window, yelled, "Sam? C'mon up."

I did it the hard way. Leapt to a garbage can, up to the awning that shades the back door, then up to Spike's window.

"Show-off," he said.

"Like you," I said flatly, "when you talk about antique furniture and art."

His apartment was neat. Donna, his roommate, the reporter for the *Post*, had a taste for high-tech. No clutter, no frills. Her taste was the absolute opposite of Spike's and the one sticky point in their domestic relationship.

"So." Spike settled on a black metal shelf the same color as his coat. "I described the bald burglar and Sugary'd never seen him. Your turn," he said.

"How about some lunch?"

"Ah," he said. "Sugary owed you a can of tuna. She asked me to deliver it."

"And did you?"

"Not yet. But I did get it open."

Donna has a high-tech electric opener. Spike opens cans for me, often for a flat ten percent of the contents.

Considering the fact that he'd worked for me this morning, he demanded twelve percent.

Considering how much he'd apparently enjoyed it, we compromised at nine.

"Memorial Day weekend," Spike said as we were eating. "Do you think that's important?"

"I don't know," I said. "Why?"

"Well . . . it's the weekend the Crandles moved in and the Sternwoods left town."

"Close," I said, "but wrong. The Sternwoods didn't *leave* on Memorial Day weekend, they redecorated."

"Oh."

We were sitting on a white metal desk in the bedroom. Spike searched around on the desktop for a pencil and stuck it in his mouth, which made him look thoughtful.

"Fuffnichuf muffuff," he said around the pencil.

"Absolutely," I told him. "I couldn't agree more."

He laughed and dropped the pencil. "Furniture movers. Same guy that moved in the Crandles' furniture also moved some new stuff in for the Sternwoods. How's that for a theory?"

I thought for a second. "Okay," I said, "but what about the Kellys and the Cohens?"

"Right." He looked suddenly dejected. "I forgot."

"Hey buddy. If you really want to be a detective — you remember the first rule?"

He narrowed his eyes at me. "Never Assume?"

"Exactly," I nodded. "Never assume you're right, but also, on the other hand —"

"Never assume you're wrong?"

"Exactly." I nodded. "So let's check it out."

Back in the sixties, before they stopped using the dumbwaiter to haul garbage, they made it automatic with buttons, from "B" to "12," for the floors.

As I've said, there are twenty-four apartments in the building, meaning two to a floor. The dumbwaiter shaft runs between the two kitchens and each of the kitchens has a doorway to the shaft.

"Okay," I said to Spike as we were riding up to eight, "you take the Kellys', I'll take the Cohens'."

"And we look for new furniture?"

"That and something else."

He frowned. "And what else?"

I shrugged. "I don't know."

"Ah-hah!" he said. "Sam's second rule of detection."

"Exactly." I grinned at him. "Never just look for what you're looking for."

"Right."

"Rule number two," I said, "is Keep An Open Mind."

The dumbwaiter stopped.

Spike took the door on the left to the Kellys', and I took the door on the right to the Cohens'.

13

When I lived at the precinct, the guy who taught me most about being a detective was Detective Ricardo.

Rick was pretty old and getting ready to retire. He was spending his final six months at the precinct doing something at a desk. I never figured out just exactly what he did, but he did it on the nightwatch — midnight to eight.

The job wasn't thrilling and the night was pretty long so he talked to me a lot.

He liked to complain about the hot dog detectives.

"You know what a hot dog detective is, Sammy? I'll explain it like this: On the one hand, you got your hot dogs. On the other hand, you got your cool cats. You follow what I'm saying? Your dogs are impatient, your cats are laid back. Your dogs are fighters, your cats are observers."

He paused for a second and looked me in the eye.

"For example: Put a dog and a cat in a kitchen. A flat second later, ask the dog what it saw and the dog'll say 'food.' Ask the cat what it saw and a half an hour later that cat is still talking.

"Remember that," he said. "And remember that everything you see can be a clue."

I thought about Rick as I landed very softly on the Cohens' kitchen floor and then looked around the room.

The kitchen had blue-flowered paper on the walls that was dotted with a number of child-sized fingerprints, some made in peanut butter, some made in jam. A couple of drawings were taped to the refrigerator. One was a seven-headed dragon, signed *BILLY*. The other was a whale (or a pickle) signed *BO*.

Bo and Billy were six-year-old twins.

I looked at the clock.

It was 4:35.

Spike had said Billy and Bo went to day camp and stayed till five o'clock when Mrs. Cohen picked them up.

Good. I had plenty of time to look around.

I looked at the kitchen. There were dishes in the sink with the general leavings of four peoples' breakfasts. Corn muffin crumbs made a trail across the floor. I tested them for staleness. They were older than breakfast by at least seven hours. A midnight muffin, I decided. Very nice.

I followed the corn muffin trail through the dining room (no new funiture, peach-colored walls) and continued to track it through a peach-colored hall.

I tracked it to the living room and up to the sofa where it ended abruptly in a large pile of books. Mr. Cohen, I remembered, was a history professor. His wife was a potter. She made a lot of pots.

There were pots on the windowsills and pots on the floor. There were flowers in some of them, and plants and a lot of different herbs in the others.

The rug was Indian. The furniture was tan. A guitar sat upright in a cozy-looking chair; the rug seemed to double as a car racing track. About a dozen model cars stood frozen, mid-race.

I was looking around me at the fresh, very clean-looking peach-colored walls when Spike hollered, "Sam?"

I turned and then stared.

Spike, who's ordinarily black, was all white.

"What happened?"

He looked at me darkly. "Three guesses."

I grinned. "You had a terrible shock and turned gray."

He shook his head rapidly and fine silky powder seemed to fly around his face.

"Ah-hah," I said, watching it descend. "Mrs. Kelly."

He nodded.

"— was baking?"

"She was baking," he agreed. "I walked through the kitchen and she didn't even see me. I checked the apartment."

"And?"

"Read my lips."

I squinted momentarily and tried to find his lips. "No . . . new . . . *furniture*?" I said.

"Right," he said. "None. Also, I remembered to keep an open mind."

"And?"

"An open mind is very dangerous," he said. "I mean things can come into it but things can fall out. As it happens, the thing that fell *out* of my mind was —"

"Ah! That Mrs. Kelly —"

"—was baking," he said. "She saw me and screamed and then threw a cup of flour."

I laughed.

"You've got a cruel sense of humor," Spike said.

"Listen, kid," I told him, "detective work is dirty." Again, I looked around me at the fresh, very clean-looking peach-colored walls. "You check the furniture and I'll check the rest."

The walls were a blank. No pictures, no hooks. A couple of paintings were stacked against a chair.

Maybe, just maybe, I decided, they were new.

I examined the paintings. The subjects of all of them were pots filled with flowers. And every single one of them was signed *Irma Cohen, 1981.*

"This sofa" — Spike peered out from underneath the couch — "is eleven years old. And the dust underneath it is about the same age." He shrugged. "I'm just kidding, but I'd say it's seven weeks." He coughed. "Maybe eight."

I checked the terrace door while Spike went courageously off to check the bedrooms.

Actually, I liked the apartment very much. The living room was lived in — happily, comfortably, cheerfully, I thought. A family lived here and I wondered if they ever thought of bringing in a cat.

I looked at the door frame, the glass, and the lock. Once again it was obvious the door wasn't jimmied. But right there next to it — right beside the door — was a peach-colored picture hook nailed against the wall. And dangling from the hook by a ribbon was a key.

A skeleton key.

A skeleton key is a long skinny key. An ordinary key has a lot of little teeth. A skeleton key has one, maybe two. Meaning, for openers, it's easy to copy.

Logically, it had to be the key to the terrace.

But rule number one remained, "Never Assume."

I squinted at the key. The jump — maybe three-and-a-half feet — was no sweat. But getting that ribbon off the hook was something else.

I hurled myself up and tried to grab it with my teeth and went skittering to the floor.

It took eleven more tries, and then finally I did it.

Spike, coming in at the eleventh, said, "Wow!"

"Never mind about wow." I was looking at the key. I examined it closely and saw that it was flecked with little bright yellow dots.

I touched them. They were sticky.

I tasted them. "Wax."

Spike trotted over. "Wax?" he said.

"Wax. Like in candle wax, Spike." I grinned. "So we know how Mr. Quark got the key."

"Perhaps" — Spike looked at me — "*some* of us know, but then some of us — no."

I explained about wax. That you can buy it in sheets about the size of a postcard. "You'd warm it, get it soft, and then you'd press the key into it and presto! The shape of the key is in the wax."

"And then what?"

"You'd take it to a locksmith," I said. "You'd say, 'Copy this shape.' "

Spike started laughing. Then he got excited and raced around the room, getting flour over everything.

"*And* —" he said, racing from the sofa to the chair, "*and* —" he said, jumping from the window to the wall, "once you had the key to the Cohens' terrace door, you'd also have the key to the Kellys' and the Crandles'."

"*What?*" I said.

He suddenly halted in his tracks, looking sober, intelligent, and once again black.

"Sorry," he said, "but if I'd shaken that flour off in Donna's place, she'd kill me. Here" — he looked down — "it sort of mingles with the dust."

"The key," I said impatiently.

"All the terrace doors have the same lock and key. Trust me," he said. "Donna lost her key once and borrowed Mrs. Brown's."

I was thinking that over when I heard a little *click*.

From where we were standing, we could see the front door and we could hear well beyond it.

A key started jingling. A voice said, "Billy-Bo, go wash your hands. Bo-Billy, wash your face."

Clack! The door opened and we headed for the dumbwaiter faster than a shot.

*   *   *

When I got to the bookstore, the office was deserted. The desk held another cup of coffee and some cake, and the radio was playing — my favorite Brandenburg concerto by Bach.

My corduroy pillow looked soft and inviting. I climbed to the bookshelf and thought about Rick. *"Remember,"* he'd told me, *"remember that everything you see can be a clue."*

I was trying to remember everything I'd seen as I yawned uncontrollably and settled into bed.

Dustballs and flowerpots,
Dishes and crumbs.
When the details are boring
The mind quickly numbs. . . .

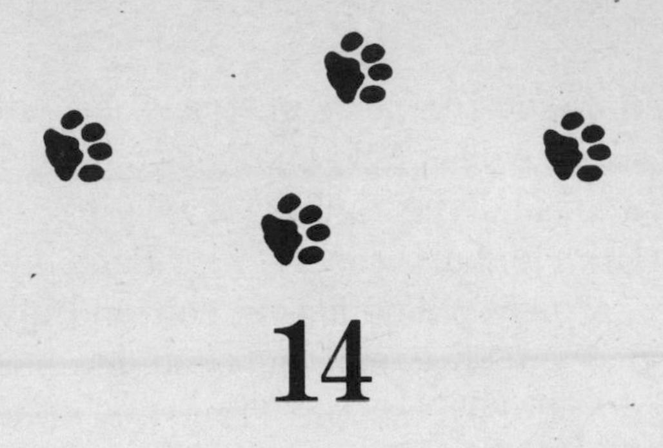

14

Tuesday dawned hot, cloudy, and humid. The address I'd been given for Sandy — the guy who'd been robbed July fourth — turned out to be in NoHo, south of the Village and a little to the east. A friendly neighborhood of tenements and lofts and shops and cafes.

The place I was looking for was Candlewick Studios. "It isn't where he lives," Sue had said, "it's where he works."

I asked her what he did and she'd looked at me as though I were dumber than a stone.

"Sandy?" she said. "He's Peter."

"Uh-huh." I nodded. "So why have we been calling him Sandy?"

"Because," she said patiently, "Sandy's his name, but you asked me what he does and what he *does* is Peter."

I continued to look blank.

"He's an actor," she exploded. "He's Peter!"

It dawned. "You mean Peter-the-Picky-Eater?"

"Hooray," she said, applauding. "Sometimes you're slow but you eventually arrive."

Peter-the-Picky-Eater — as everyone who's smarter than a rock garden knows — is the star of a series of Catslop commercials. Peter turns his nose up at warm roasted chicken, at solid white tuna, at tender strips of calves liver gently cooked with bacon, even boned Dover sole. What he goes for is Catslop — a food so disgusting, so entirely repellent, it looks like it was something pre-eaten by a goat and rejected into a can.

On the other hand, pretending to like it pays well. Sandy apparently supported his family — kept them in a glitzy Fifth Avenue condo with a lot of toys and treats.

Candlewick Studios was set on the corner of a cobblestone street. A three-story building with a wide red door held open with a chain.

An anteroom led to another open door, which led to the studio — a large dark room. Dark around the edges but bright in the middle. A battery of lights — about 10,000 watts — was focused on an elegant dining room table full of candlesticks and flowers.

A television camera — something like an overgrown robot on wheels — stood obediently by while a short heavy man in a loud Hawaiian shirt barked orders at the crew.

"Okay, everybody. Quiet on the set." He settled in a green canvas chair marked DIRECTOR. "Sandy? We're ready for Sandy and the shrimp."

A woman came in and put a large plate of shrimp in the center of the table.

"Okay, where's Sandy?"

"He's coming," said a voice as a green-eyed, sandy-haired, rugged-looking cat hurtled neatly to the table where he sprawled, looking bored.

He was nearly too handsome. Too shiny, too sleek, too lean and athletic, with hard high cheekbones and a flat straight nose. He was one of those guys who gets his picture on greeting cards and calendars, I thought. A real lady-killer, too.

"Sandy?" The director started pacing as he talked. "Okay, that's your cue. When she calls you for supper, I want you to lie there just the way you are, with your eyes closed tight. Then open one eye, look up at her darkly, as though to say, 'Lady, forget it with the fish,' and then yawn, close the eye. Get it? Okay, everybody, let's roll."

A woman rushed up to the camera with a board (CATSLOP, it said, SCENE 2, TAKE 1) and then hit it with a stick. After that, it was quiet enough to hear a pin drop.

From somewhere in the shadows a soft crooning voice said, "Peterkins. Supper."

Sandy was perfect. He opened one eye, looked meanly at the shadow, appeared to show a desperate contempt for the shrimp, yawned, closed the eye.

"That's a print," someone said.

The director said, "Cut. Okay, that's a print." The lights went out. "Coffee break," he said, and everybody headed for a table at the back.

Sandy yawned lazily and rose from the tablecloth, stretched like he was posing for a fashion magazine, and then pounced on the shrimp.

I moved up beside him. "Nice going," I said.

He looked at me. "Tell me you're not a reporter."

"Easy," I told him. "I'm not a reporter."

I explained who I was and exactly what I wanted.

"Oh yeah. July fourth," he said, chomping on a shrimp. "Little dude cleaned us out." He gestured at the dinner bowl. "Have some," he said. "You want some catnip or something?"

"I'm working," I told him.

"Tough," he said, "huh? I mean, you work like a dog, a little burglar takes it all."

"He take anything from you?"

"You mean personally? No. It's my managers he robbed. Only where do you think they got the bread to buy the jewels?"

I nodded sympathetically.

"Catslop," he said. "With the world the way it is, you gotta eat a lot of Catslop just to get by."

"Do you?" I said. "I mean, actually eat it?"

He looked at me and grinned. "I'm an actor," he said. "I only act like I'm eating it. After the commercial I can puddle all over it and bury it in sand."

The director started hollering, "Five minutes, folks."

"About the burglary," I said, and described the bald burglar. Sandy'd never seen him — a fact that was something of a mystery in itself. Here was this guy who'd been to everybody's house, except nobody'd ever seen him. I confirmed that he'd stolen a thirty-carat diamond and a Patek Phillipe.

"And he entered through the terrace?"

"Absolutely," Sandy said. "We got home the day after and the door was on the floor."

I squinted. "On the floor?"

"He busted it. He cut the thing clean out of its frame."

I thought about it slowly. "Had you recently changed the lock?"

Sandy cocked his head. "About . . . six weeks before. How'd you know that?" he said.

"I didn't. But the pattern is, he's always had the key. And a smell," I said suddenly. "You notice any smell?"

"Like what?" He looked alert.

"Like floor wax," I said. "Only nastier. A little like bug-killer, too."

"That's it," he said. "He tracked it directly from the terrace and straight to the dresser. And it really made me nuts. I mean . . . I'm pretty certain I'd smelled the stuff before. But where . . . ?" He made a shrug.

The director yelled, "Hey, people! Let's roll some film."

There was general stirring.

"If you think of it," I said, "call Sue and leave a message."

He nodded. "Will do."

The director yelled, "Ready for Sandy and the slop!"

I grinned and then offered in a grating falsetto: "Peterkins. Supper."

Sandy rolled his eyes.

15

I walked north on Broadway under dark, leaden skies. At Bleecker Street I turned west and then headed towards the greenery of Washington Square Park. It was a long hot walk but it wasn't lonely and it wasn't boring. There's nothing boring about the streets.

Loud crowds of children wearing cutoffs and running shoes streamed around the sidewalks. Fast boys on bicycles zipped around the curbs as though traffic lights and crosswalks hadn't been invented and the world belonged to bikes.

Stationed near the gutter were peddlers of all kinds — some of them with carts and some of them with blankets spread flat across the ground. The carts held apples, and books without covers, and watches that didn't work. The blankets held pottery and jewelry and socks. And other folks, with nothing to peddle, held cups along with handwritten signs, I'M HUNGRY AND HOMELESS; I'M HUNGRY AND SICK.

These are complicated times. The fat get fatter and the lean get leaner and crime, like dandelions, blossoms in the gap.

When I got to the bookstore, it was twenty after seven and rain was in the air. The office was stifling. The air conditioner was off, the windows were shut tight, the radio was silent, and the only food in sight was a bowl of dry cereal without any milk. And the telephone was ringing.

I stepped on the speaker button. "Sam here," I said.

"Well of course you're there, Sam. You couldn't answer if you weren't."

"Sugary," I said. "I'm hot and I'm hungry and I'm not in the mood for jokes. Can I call you back later?"

"If you want my opinion, Sam, you should have called me sooner. I mean" — she sounded pouty — "you take a girl's number, not to mention her tuna fish, and never even call?"

"I apologize," I said.

"Do you mean it?"

"Sincerely."

"Good." She hung up.

I sat there for a second and listened to the dial

tone and slowly shook my head. I admit that I've solved a lot of mysteries in my life but girls aren't one of them.

Why had she suddenly, abruptly hung up?

I turned on the air conditioner, scratched my head thoroughly, and settled down to think.

The dumbwaiter whined; the door popped open, and there stood Sugary — a large slice of anchovy pizza at her feet.

I grinned at her. "Sugary, you're one swell client." I helped her unload it and get it to the desk. "Have you already eaten?"

She nodded. "Go on. I'll just ask you a few questions."

"Shoot." I went digging for the anchovies first.

"Okay," she said. "I only want to ask you where you've been, and what you've been doing, and what you've discovered, and what it adds up to, and what you're gonna do."

"Uh-huh," I said, chewing on a fish. "Is that all?"

"Did I miss something?"

"Nope. I think you just about covered it."

"So," she said. "Tell."

I ate silently for a time while I tried to figure out just exactly what I knew and just exactly what it meant. I felt suddenly depressed. For everything I'd learned, I hadn't gained any knowledge. Facts aren't knowledge. Or at least they aren't knowledge till they start to add up — make a point, tell a story.

I explained that to Sugary who said she didn't care.

"Okay," I said. "Fact: Mr. Quark is the burglar. He's a male human being with a bald top of the head and a fringe of brown hair."

"Where's the hair?" Sugary said.

"Ear to ear across the back."

"Go on," she said.

"Fact: In the last seven weeks he's robbed nine sets of people — or nine that I know of — five of which I've checked. The three in this building plus the Sternwoods and Sandy."

"Sandy?" Sugary said. "You don't — I mean, you don't mean *the* Sandy, do you? The movie star?"

I nodded.

"Oh Sam!" Her eyes widened and her paw flew to her face. "You really, really met Sandy?"

"In the fur," I said. "Yes."

"Oh Sam." She danced around. "What's he really, really like? I mean really. Is he handsome? Is he nice?"

"He's okay," I said, eating. "Hey look. You want to talk about Sandy or the case?"

"About Sandy." She giggled. "Okay, about the case."

"Fact," I said sternly. "He begins on the roof

and breaks in through the terrace. Fact," I said, thinking of the list I got from Tom. "From the cases I know about, he goes to visit Cheater exactly the next day. In fact —"

I stopped talking. I switched the computer on and typed the word *Jade.*

The list popped out at me: the dates of Quark's visits.

June 7	11:45 PM
June 14	12 midnight
June 21	11:30 PM
June 28	11:40 PM
July 5	11:30 PM
July 12	11:50 PM
July 20	12:30 AM

I stared at it and grinned. "That's it," I said. "We got him."

"We do?" she said. "How?"

"There's a pattern here. Look. He visited Cheater not exactly the next day but exactly the next *night.* At approximately midnight, give or take an hour."

"So?" she said.

"*So,*" I said, "look at the calendar, Sugary. Or do some arithmetic. Look. June seventh — first visit — was a Sunday. There are seven days in a week. Seven plus seven is what?"

"Fourteen?"

"Next visit," I said, "was June fourteenth."

"A Sunday."

"Very good. Add seven."

"Twenty-first?"

"Third visit, twenty-first. Can you figure out the pattern?"

She sat down next to me and stared at the computer. Her mouth moved slightly. Once in a while she counted on her nails.

"Oh," she said abruptly. "He's visited Cheater every single Sunday for the last seven weeks."

"Exactly," I beamed.

"So?" she said.

"*So?* You're asking me a so? Sugary, Sugary. He's visited Cheater every single Sunday for the last seven weeks. *So*," I said, "the odds remain exceptionally good that he'll also visit Cheater *next* Sunday night."

"Oh!" she said. "Oh, you are brilliant beyond belief."

"So," I said. "Sunday night I'll stake out the Kit-Kat. This time I'll follow him."

"I got it," Sugary said. "You'll follow him to his house —"

"— Where I think he's got the jade."

"Oh Sam!" She started grabbing me and jumping up and down. "You're a genius! You're an angel! You're the very best detective in the whole entire world!"

I said, "Don't overdo it."

The dumbwaiter whined. Spike popped out and looked from Sugary to me. "I thought I heard the sounds of untrammeled jubilation. What's up?"

I glanced at Sugary. "Don't get her started."

Sugary started anyway. The telephone was ringing and I picked it up quickly. "Sam here," I said.

And before the call was over, my terrific plans for Sunday were moldering in the grave.

16

"Sammy? It's Tom."

I swiveled in my chair. In front of me, Sugary was bubbling to Spike who was watching her with wry but enchanted amusement. I pointed at the pizza and offered some to Spike. "Tom, what's happening?"

"Much," he said.

"Go."

"About six o'clock tonight I was sitting in the window and Quark passes by."

I felt myself tense. "Did you tail him?"

"Directly to the Apple Cafe. He took a table on the sidewalk. I snuck right under it and caught the whole scene."

"And?"

"He met a guy. This guy — if you're ready — was a fence from L.A. Quark made a deal. He'll sell the guy the jade and something — I think he said a Rumplemeyer — Sunday."

"Sunday?" I said.

"This Sunday at noon."

"Where?"

"He didn't say but his buddy seemed to know."

"Did you tail him from the Apple?"

There was silence on the line.

"I blew it," Tom said. "I lost him and the next thing I know he's in a cab."

This time the agonizing silence was mine.

"I'm really sorry," Tom said.

"Hey forget it. You were great. See you later, Tom. Thanks."

Slowly, I pivoted back to face the desk.

Spike and Sugary were watching me, alert.

"What happened?" Spike said.

"Nothing." I tried to sound calm, cool and brilliant. "Nothing," I said, "except we're back to square one."

17

Wednesday it rained. A howling wind threw water against the windows like a big angry fist hurling pebbles against the panes.

Hunnicker was grouchy and appeared to have a cold. He settled at the desk chair, clicked on the miniature Sony in the cabinet, and watched an old movie.

The day was a washout.

I moved from the office and paced the empty store, its walls lined with tales about the world's great detectives: Sam Spade, Philip Marlowe, Sherlock Holmes, Nancy Drew.

And here I was, stuck. My own story ended at chapter seventeen.

There was nothing more to do. At least nothing I could think of.

How could I find Quark? I knew what he looked like but I didn't know who he was. I didn't know his actual name or his address. And even his description didn't do me any good. It could fit about a quarter of the men in Manhattan.

I moved to the front window and staked out the rain. It was bouncing off the sidewalks, splattering off the walls.

On another kind of day, in another kind of mood, I would have relished all the rain. I'd have sat here reading, feeling comfortable and dry.

Today I felt restless. Uncomfortable. Caged.

Down to business, I told myself. Think, think, think.

I squinted at the rain.

Okay, I thought slowly. If the pattern was a pattern — Saturday night robberies, Sunday night sales — then probably, possibly, Quark would go out again *this* Saturday night.

Swell. Did that help me?

No. Not a bit.

The question, of course, would be *where* would he strike, and I couldn't hope to know.

And by Sunday at noon the whole ball game was over. The jade would be gone. And with it, the evidence that Max was in the clear.

What I needed was a break. What I needed was a hot hard burst of inspiration.

What I needed, short of that, was a nice long nap.

18

Thursday was sunny. Not only sunny, but actually nice: seventy-eight degrees, not humid, good breeze.

It was either the breeze that awakened me or Sue going *psst!* from the window, or maybe just a dream.

I blinked and saw Sue — her honey-colored hair looking spangled by the sun.

"Up, up!" she said. "We're going on a picnic in the trees."

I looked at her and yawned. I'd been awake half the night, tossing on my bed and chasing thoughts around the ceiling till they'd mingled with the dawn.

I stretched and then moaned.

"Up, up!" she said, a honeycomb streaking through the window. Leaping to the bookshelf. Tickling my stomach, going, "Up, up, up!"

I was helpless in her paws.

"Hey, look — I'm in a terrible mood," I said, laughing.

"I know," she said. "You're working too hard. You need to play."

"But I can't," I said, laughing.

"But you can," she said, tickling.

"I surrender," I conceded and tumbled onto the floor.

A couple of minutes later, I found myself reluctantly trotting out to the street. The weather, I was forced to admit, was superb.

"But I'm not staying long," I said.

"I thought you surrendered."

"That was then," I said, blinking at the sun, "this is now."

We'd turned onto Tenth Street and headed for the park.

"But you're wrong," she said. "You've got to let your mind get some air. My mother used to say —"

"You're quoting your *mother*?"

"My mother used to say, 'If you let your mind wander, it'll bury you with fish.' "

I looked at her. "Sue, that makes no sense at all."

"That's why I never quote my mom," she said dryly. "Actually" — she paused — "I think it means something like . . . well . . . like your mind'll come back with something good."

"Uh-huh," I said. "Speaking of the mind bringing fish . . . " I pointed at the big yellow sign across the street:

SINGE & O'MALLEY'S
CHOWDER HOUSE & GRILLE
OPEN FOR LUNCH 12:30 P.M.

I was already picturing a thick creamy chowder, not to mention O'Malley, who's a sucker for a cat. I suggested we stick around and wait till 12:30. Sue said she'd counted on a picnic in the trees.

"You want a tree?" I said, pointing at a tree. "There's a tree."

She checked out the tree. It was solid and leafy — a street-smart tree that survived against the odds. She agreed to a compromise and leapt, with the swiftness of a bird, up the bark.

I jumped up beside her and sprawled on a fat limb.

For a time we said nothing, just lay there contentedly and sunned among the leaves.

Sue started purring. "Are you letting your mind wander?"

"Mmm," I said. "Look at those idiots on the street."

She looked where I pointed. There were two men arguing. One of them was carrying a ladder from a house and the other one was hollering, "I said I wanted yellow!"

"That's yellow," said the first.

"If that's yellow," yelled the yeller, "then daffodils are blue!"

The guy with the ladder threw a bag into the garbage pail and hurried into a truck. He rolled down the window. "Get your eyes fixed," he shrieked. *Zip-zoom*, he drove away.

Sue looked at me and laughed.

"Come on," I said. "The door to O'Malley's just opened."

We hurried down the street. And then suddenly I stopped. There was something in the air and it wasn't red herring.

I sniffed, sniffed again. "Do you smell that?" I said.

She looked at me. "I smell about ninety million things."

I sniffed, looked around. What I saw was the garbage pail we'd spotted from the tree. And the smell I was smelling was the strong and decidedly strange smell of Quark.

I circled the garbage pail. Right. That was it. "Hey Red," I said. "C'mere."

She said, "Don't call me —"

"Just close your eyes," I said impatiently, "and tell me what you smell."

Sue closed her eyes. "Something like floor wax only nastier," she said. "Like bug-killer, too."

"That's it," I said. "Quark."

In one nimble movement I jumped onto the garbage pail and squinted into the mess. Sitting on the top of it were paint-spattered rags — a kind of green-yellow paint — and a gray metal can that said TURPENTINE on it.

"Turpentine!" I hollered. "Quark smells of turpentine."

"Turpentine?"

"Turpentine. Paint thinner, Susie."

"And don't call me —"

"Listen — he's a painter, okay?"

"You mean a house painter?"

"Sure. He gets paint on his sneakers and he has to clean it off."

"With turpentine?"

"Right. C'mon," I said, running. "Let's eat and get to work."

19

"A house painter?" Spike looked up at me and blinked. We sat on his terrace. I'd discovered him sleeping on a *Times* editorial and whimpering in his sleep. He yawned rather openly and tried to disguise it by pretending to say "Ah."

"I didn't ask you for an *Ah.* It's just a theory," I conceded. I paced around the tiles. "But theoretically, it works. I mean, nobody sticks around when there's a painter in the house. At least, not in the same room."

"You got a point," he said. "A painter wants to snoop, he can snoop."

"And we know," I said slowly, "that the Crandles got painted."

"Okay," he said. "We know because Crandle told McFee. But on the other paw, Sammy —" He paused. "I hate to mention this, but what about the others?"

"I don't know about the others. I don't know about the Kellys but I know about the Cohens."

I was thinking about Rick. Rick and his everything-you-see-can-be-a-clue.

I was thinking of the very clean peach-colored walls in the otherwise less than immaculate apartment — a house full of dustballs, fingerprints and crumbs.

I was thinking of the trio of nicely framed pictures that were stacked against the chair, and the walls without hooks, and how usually a painter pulls the hooks before he paints.

"Hey — nice thinking." Spike looked at me and frowned. After a breath, he said, "I think I've got a hunch."

"About the Kellys?"

"And their kitchen."

"Go on."

"It was white. I mean very, very white. I mean *very*, very white."

"Like it was painted."

"Like that."

We grinned at each other.

"Okay." I started kicking a pebble across the tile. "Not switching the subject, there's a funny shade of red — something like a cross between cinnamon and catsup —"

"Called cinnabar," he said.

"Okay, so the Sternwoods' living room was cinnabar. Before they re-did it, the living room was French."

"Okay, what's your question?"

"Okay, Mr. Expert. Is cinnabar French?"

He grinned at me. "Its other name is Chinese Red. Does that answer you?"

Click! All the pieces came together. When the Sternwoods converted from French to Chinese, their apartment had been painted. And I even knew when: Memorial Day weekend.

What I needed now was Sandy.

I borrowed Spike's telephone, looked up the number, and reached him at his condo. He answered with a growl.

"If I woke you, too bad," I said. "I need to ask a question. Just one. Were you painted?"

He yawned. "How'd you know?"

"Turpentine," I said.

It woke him like a shot. "Ah-hah!" he said thoughtfully. "So *that's* where I'd smelled it. It was sickening. It hung around the air here for days."

"Did you ever see the painter?"

"Not me, man. I work. After work, I went to Sue's."

I drummed on the table. "Did you stay there for dinner?"

He laughed at me. "Don't get your back up, ole buddy. I left about six. In time to come home to a nice smelly house."

I could have said thank-you-good-bye and hung up, but I found myself asking him to pin down the date.

He put me on hold while he hunted for his book.

I looked suddenly at Spike. "Ask Sugary," I said, "what date she was painted."

Spike nodded happily and bounded out of the room.

Sandy came back and said, "May twenty-second."

It was then I said thank-you-good-bye and hung up and then dialed another number.

Half a dozen rings and then, "Sternwood residence."

"Lady Anne?" I said. "Sam. What date were you painted?"

"I?" she said, "have never been painted in my life. I'm a natural blonde, dear, as everybody knows."

I rephrased the question.

"Oh," she said. "Hmm. Well, I don't know the number, dear, I only know the name."

"The name?" I said.

"Friday. Like in *Robinson Crusoe*?"

I glanced at Donna's date book. The Friday of

Memorial Day weekend — I found it — was Friday the 29th. And Sandy had also been painted on a Friday. Friday the 22nd. I grinned like a fool and said, "Thank you, Lady Anne. You've been very, very helpful."

"Oh dear," she said. "I don't like to think of myself as helpful. It sounds so . . . tacky. Could you change that to generous?"

"Of course," I said. "You're very, very generous, Lady Anne."

Spike came in as I was getting off the line.

"Sugary said Friday. It was Friday, June fifth."

"Thank you, Lord Spike. You are generous to a fault."

At 6:07 I was back at my computer. I typed:

NAME OF PERSON	DAY PAINTED	DAY ROBBED

Then I filled in the list:

Sandy	(Fri) May 22	(Sat) July 4
Lady Anne	(Fri) May 29	(Sat) July 11
Sugary	(Fri) June 5	(Sat) July 18
X	?	(Sat) July 25

If my theory was correct, then "X" (meaning "person or persons unknown") would be robbed in two days — the upcoming Saturday, July 25th.

If I was doubly correct, then X had been painted.

I was looking for a pattern. If I figured out *when* Mr. X had been painted, then possibly, with luck, I'd figure out who he was.

I looked at the calendar and looked at the list. Then suddenly I had it. Mr. X had been painted on

(Fri) June 12

20

Sue's green eyes looked directly into mine. "I don't get it, Sam," she said.

I repeated my conclusion: The apartments had been painted exactly six weeks and one day before the hit. If that continued as the pattern, then "X" — who'd get burgled on July 25th — had been painted June 12th. It came down to arithmetic.

Sue shook her head. "First of all, what about the Kellys and the Cohens?"

I grinned at her. I'd already interviewed Panda, the Manx on the 8th floor. According to Panda, the Cohens and the Kellys had been painted the same day and the day was June 5th. "Same day as Sugary."

Sue cocked her head. "By the very same painter?"

"Exactly. Meany's Law is 'Do it cheap, bad and fast.' "

Sue laughed and warmed some milk.

Of the many, many things I like the most about Sue there are two tied for first. One, her intelligence and two, her sense of humor.

"Even so —" She started pacing on the ledge around the counter. "Six weeks and one day? I mean why would a guy do that? Why would a guy stick to such a dumb stupid pattern?"

I shrugged and said, "Why did the chicken cross the road?"

"Meaning?"

"I don't know. And it's possible that even the chicken didn't know. Hey listen, Sue," I said, "people've been questioning that chicken's motivation for a couple of thousand years and what difference does it make? The *point*," I said hotly, "is the chicken crossed the road and now you've got a chicken on the other side of the road and what're you gonna do about it?"

"Wow," she said.

"What?"

"I just love the way you talk. I don't always understand it —"

"Of course you do," I said.

"Of course I do," she laughed. She opened her appointment book and flipped back the pages. "Let me see if I can answer you."

"You know what I'm asking?"

"Of course I do," she said. "You're asking if I

know who was painted June twelfth."

"I adore you," I said.

Her paw skimmed the list of appointments for June 12th. "Miss Kitty." She pointed. "Miss Kitty McClintock but she likes to be called Ms. Her family sent her here to spend the afternoon."

"Same as Sandy," I said.

She looked at me and giggled. "Are you jealous?"

"Not a bit. I mean it simply occurred to me if Sandy came to visit you the day he was painted, maybe others did, too. Elementary, my dear Watson."

"Sam," she said sweetly, *"don't call me Watson!"*

21

The first obstacle was the doorman.

Sue had called Kitty to tell her I'd be coming, and Kitty had responded with elaborate instructions: Get in the elevator, ride to the top floor, take the stairway to the roof, and then leap to her terrace. She lived in the penthouse on the 17th floor.

The doorman was fierce — a gold-braided giant who was planted in the doorway with his arms across his chest. It was twenty of eleven on a bright Friday morning and he looked as though he'd stand there till the cows came home.

Spike said, "I hate to be a quitter, but I quit."

"Just be patient," I told him.

I glanced around the street. Exactly next door to this intimidating condo was its absolute opposite. A rundown buiding with a wide open doorway and a mangy-looking hall.

I motioned with my head, and we both trotted

over and squinted through the door: a cramped marble lobby, a directory on the wall.

I moved up and studied it. The building housed offices — dentists and accountants and literary agents — none of whom, I gathered, were doing very well since the lobby was deserted. I turned and looked around.

A bad-looking elevator loomed against the wall, its old-fashioned indicator stuck at "17" — the top of the building. Beside it was a door marked:

FIRE EXIT

KEEP THIS LOCKED AT ALL TIMES

The door was propped open. I peered around the frame. Ahead was a stairway. To the side was a dark and very dismal-looking window propped open with a wedge.

"C'mon," I said to Spike.

He stared. "You're not seriously suggesting that we walk?"

"I'm not suggesting, I'm walking." I started up the stairs. When I got to the eighth landing, I stopped and took a rest and heard Spike coming after me. I waited in the dark.

"Why," he said weakly, "did you want to take the stairs?"

"Because," I said thoughtfully, "the burglar's gonna take them."

"He is?"

"I don't know but I figure it's a good guess.

I'm figuring there's no one in the building on the weekend. He'd come through the window and he'd —"

"What?"

"We're gonna see."

We continued up the stairs and then suddenly, for no good reason I could name, I stopped. I smelled trouble. My ears made a tense half-circle in the air. My neck hairs stiffened. A quick cold finger played piano up my spine.

I blinked and looked up. Two floors above me, sitting on the banister's thick iron rail, was the biggest, toughest-looking cat I've ever seen.

"You outta your turf, boy." He hissed and then growled. "Turn tail or you're meat."

This cat wasn't kidding. He was twenty-five pounds' worth of tiger-striped muscle and blood-speckled teeth. I drew a long breath. Spike, right behind me, had so many hairs up he looked like a porcupine and, just for an instant there, I wished that he were.

I trotted out my best Clint Eastwood imitation: "Easy, man," I drawled. "Relax. We're just a couple of strangers passing through."

"Through the meat grinder, Bub," and with that one, he let out a Kung Fu battle cry and jetted from the rail.

He didn't know his own strength. He was aiming right at us but he picked up a tail wind that wouldn't let him go. He flew right past us like a fur-covered bullet and crumpled on the second-floor landing with a thud.

For a moment after that, there was dead, stone silence.

"Hey!" I called after him. "You still want to fight?"

Another long silence; then he whispered in a small choked soprano, "Never mind."

Spike sighed deeply. We continued on our way.

At the top of the stairway, a door labeled ROOF stood conveniently ajar.

The roof was black tar. A couple of Pepsi cans rolled around aimlessly and jingled in the breeze. There was nothing else to see except a low brick wall that made a border around the roof.

I jumped to the top of it and, just as I'd suspected, it immediately butted on the roof next door.

"Some roof," I said softly.

It was landscaped with flowers and paved with terra cotta. There were deck chairs and lounges and little glass tables with blue striped umbrellas and a grill for cooking food.

Spike came after me and whistled through his teeth. "It's a definitely yuppie rooftop," he said.

We dropped to the tiles. The roof was immense. About a million yards away, a rectangular camera was perched above a blue metal door that read STAIRS. I went close and checked it out.

"Uh-huh," I said. "Look at this. The camera takes your picture if you're coming through the door. And over there — around the door frame. Look — you see the wire?" It was tacked against the frame.

"What about it?" Spike looked at me.

"It triggers an alarm. Therefore —"

"I got it. I'm not stupid," Spike said. "Therefore the burglar isn't coming through the door and you were absolutely right."

"So it seems," I said flatly, and suddenly the airwaves exploded into sound. I gritted my teeth and Spike ran for cover as a barrel of rock music rolled across the air. A shattering, thundering aerial bombardment of hard-hearted voices and electrified guitars.

A woman's voice screached at it, "STOP THAT RACKET!"

The racket didn't stop.

I sprinted to a catwalk at the corner of the roof and looked directly at the noise. Its obvious source was a twelve-year-old boy on the terrace right below, sprawled on a blanket with a radio on his chest. At the corner of his terrace, a frantic and incredibly distressed-looking cat held her paws across her ears.

"YOU EITHER STOP IT THIS INSTANT OR I'M CALLING THE POLICE. I'M VERY SERIOUS, YOUNG MAN!"

The young man didn't move. He lay with his eyes closed tightly to the sun. Then slowly his fingers sort of twitched around the dial. The music got softer.

"C'mon," I said to Spike.

We dropped to the terrace. The cat who'd been standing there streaked through a cat door and motioned for us to follow.

The living room was small and surprisingly modest. The cat who was facing us was motherly and brown with very wide hazel eyes.

"You don't know what it's been like here," she said by way of greeting. "It's been rock around the clock. You're Sam," she said efficiently. "And you, I guess, are Spike. If you boys want to look around for burglars, go ahead, only don't disturb the babies."

I looked at the babies. There were seven of them, bunking in a box marked BREAKABLE, THIS SIDE UP.

Experience has taught me if you're looking at a boxful of anybody's babies, you'd better say, "Beautiful," or otherwise you're dead.

"Very beautiful," I said.

She beamed me a look of such warm loving pride, I was even glad I'd said it.

"So they are." She kept smiling. "And a mighty lot of work. You know, being a single mother, that's a busy thing to do."

"And Sue told you why we're here?"

"Seems so," she said, wandering in circles around the box. "Long as that burglar doesn't catnap the babies, then it's all right with me."

"Will you be home?" I said.

"Saturday? No, we'll be away."

I looked suddenly at Spike who'd been marching around the room. He'd leapt to a table and was staring in wonder at a small wooden box. "What's the matter?" I said quickly.

"That," he said, pointing at the box, "is a matter of exceptional importance."

"I'll bite," I said. "Why?"

It looked, on the surface, like an ordinary box made of dark polished wood.

"It's a music box," he said. "Seventeenth century and very, very rare."

"Uh-huh." I looked away. I didn't care about the box. I was suddenly stricken with a sharp pang of doubt. I'd had everything figured: That Quark would come here. That he'd come here Saturday. Even that he'd enter through the building next door. Only what if I was wrong? It was all just air — a theory arrived at on a ladder of assumptions. And my own first principle was Never Assume.

Spike blathered on: "I believe there are only a hundred in existence. All of them made by the same Swiss craftsman."

I still didn't care. What I needed was a good solid piece of information — a clue that would tell me I was on the right track.

"Sebastian Rumplemeyer," Spike said with awe.

I turned and looked up at him. "Say that again."

"Sebastian Rumplemeyer?"

I nodded.

"Coming up: Sebastian Rumplemeyer, Sebastian Rumplemeyer, Sebastian Rumplemeyer, Sebastian —"

"Rumplemeyer," I said. "Quark told the dealer he'd be selling him the jade and something called a Rumplemeyer. Sunday afternoon."

"Then it's this one," Spike said. "Most of the others are in Italy and France."

I looked at Ms. Kitty. "I think," I said urgently, "we need to make a plan."

"As long as it doesn't hurt my little ones," she said, "it's all right with me."

22

There's a framed cartoon in Hunnicker's office: A couple of convicts sitting in a jail cell with fifty-foot walls. There's a window in the cell but it's small, thickly barred, and it's somewhere near the ceiling — a probable forty-eight feet from the ground. So there they are, the two of them, chained to the bunk, and one of them seriously says to the other one:

"Now — here's the plan . . ."

On Friday afternoon, I felt just like those guys.

Like *both* of those guys.

A part of me saying, "Now — here's the plan," and the other part saying, "Are you out of your tree? We're stuck, man. There isn't any plan that's gonna work."

I paced around the bookstore and looked for inspiration.

I needed a plan that would:

1. Catch Quark.
2. Clear Max.
3. Get the jade.

But it wasn't that simple (if you'd call that simple). Getting Max out of trouble would involve the police. So to add to my troubles, there was

4. Get police.

I looked at the clock. It was 4:57 on Friday afternoon. I had thirty-two hours to come up with something good. Saturday at midnight was the Quarking Hour.

I climbed up the ladder, examining the various volumes on the shelves. The classic, intellectual armchair detectives — the guys who caught criminals while sitting in their chairs — had nothing to offer me and nothing to say. Chairs didn't have any place in this game. It was no game for chairs.

I paced to the door again and squinted at the corner marked ACTION/ADVENTURE.

Yeah. What I needed was some ACTION/ADVENTURE.

What I needed . . .

It came to me almost in a flash.

"The reason I called you here —" I said in my officially businesslike tone.

Oscar interrupted me by holding up his paw. There were seven of us sitting on the blue velvet love seat in the courtyard in the rear. It was getting on to midnight.

"Oscar — can it wait?"

Oscar shook his head. He said, "The Fang Gang is coming."

"I'm not sure of that," I told him. "They're half an hour late."

The Fangs are a family of street-roving cats. They come from a long line of circus performers and as Wang Fang tells it, they fell off the wagon when the circus came to town. They used to be famous as The Flying Fangs — Wang, Chang, Sturm, and Drang. Talented but terribly temperamental artists.

Butch said, "Your girlfriend Angie's coming too."

I'd asked him and Jane to recruit a bunch of cats. An army, I'd told him.

Spike said, "You might as well wait a little while." He sat next to Sugary, his paw resting ever-so-gently on her back.

I shrugged and looked at Sue who said, "I think we ought to vote to give it five more minutes. All in favor, say 'I'."

There was a yammering of I's.

I paced around the court. I have to confess I have definitely mixed feelings about democracy.

When my side wins, it's a wonderful idea. When my side loses, I begin to see the virtues of absolute monarchy.

"Here they are." Spike turned and pointed at the gate. It's a seven-foot gate. But sitting on top of it were four Flying Fangs and a matted Angora.

They dropped to the courtyard with the confidence of stars.

"You're late," I said testily.

Wang made a shrug. "It's not in our contract that we have to be prompt, we just have to be good. Now I understand the terms are a slice of lox apiece. Payable Sunday."

I nodded. "That's the deal."

"It's a deal for a meal with a definite appeal." Chang tapped the rhythm of his sentence on the ground.

Drang caught the beat. "It's a good square deal for a good square meal. It's as good as a goody and as square as a —"

"Wheel!" Wang finished it and grinned up at Sturm.

Sturm looked embarrassed. "The brothers want to try to do a rap act," he said.

"Keep trying," I offered.

I looked up at Angie. "Okay?"

She said, "Fine."

Then I looked at my audience. "Now — here's the plan. . . ."

23

Saturday night it was moonless and cloudy. Dense dark shadows seemed to settle on the world. It was a night made for crime — for sneaky, spooky and extra-dark deeds.

Quark must have loved it. A burglar works better under cover of darkness, but then so do I. And as logic would have it, what's good for the cat burglar is good for the cat.

At eleven on the dot (I wasn't taking any chances) we were all in our various and well-planned positions:

Butch, Jane, and Oscar on the office-building roof.

Sue, Spike, and Sugary in Kitty's apartment.

Angie and the Fangs on the yuppie roof above.

I visited the battle stations, checking on morale.

"This waiting around is boring," Oscar said.

"If you call it a stakeout," Jane said, "it's exciting."

"No it isn't," Oscar said. "I don't care what you call it, man. Boring is boring."

"It's boring," I agreed, "but it's important, okay? You're gonna give us all a signal as soon as you see Quark."

"What's the signal?" Oscar said. "I'm so bored, I forgot."

"The signal," Butch prompted him, "is Meow-Meow-Meow."

"That's the stupidest word I ever heard," Oscar said. "This is dumb beyond belief."

Jane sighed. "Listen, Oscar. I tell you what we'll do. We'll pretend it's a cop show. You like to watch cop shows?"

"Boring," Oscar said. "I saw a cop show on Sunday. All the cops did was just chase the guy around. And around and around. In a dumb stupid circle. After a while they all collapsed in a heap."

"Oscar," Jane appealed to him, "that was no cop show, you were looking at the dryer."

"So what?" Oscar said. "Televisions, dryers, it's still the same story."

"You know?" Butch looked at me. "Oscar's got a point?"

I suggested that everybody try to relax but not enough to fall asleep.

On the roof next door, it was a totally different story: Activity. Excitement.

Chang was doing chin-ups on the television antenna. Wang practiced leaping from a table to a chair while Sturm, Drang and Angie played leapfrog on the grill.

"Okay," I said carefully, "you guys know what to do."

"Double somersault," Wang said, erupting off the chair, doing two entire circles in the middle of nowhere, and landing on the blue of a blue-and-white umbrella.

"Okay," I said happily, "you know what to do. But remember not to do it till he's on the way *out*. Out, not in."

"I got a question," Angie said. "Can I bite him on the nose?"

I shrugged. "I suppose."

"Hold it, hold it!" Chang said. "That's a rap number, brothers."

He left the antenna and landed on the tiles and started stomping out the beat: And a-ONE and a-TWO and a-ONE-ONE-TWO.

"Can I bite him on the nose till it's red like a rose, till it flows like a hose, till it drips on his clothes, till it drops to his toes, till it no longer blows, till he no longer knows if his nose is a nose? I suppose, I suppose, I suppose!"

"Oh yeah! Oh yeah-yeah-YEAH!" Angie said.

“On second thought,” I looked at them, “don’t bite his nose.”

The scene in the apartment was cozier and calm. I entered through the cat door — a small hinged panel at the bottom of the otherwise locked terrace door.

Spike was at the living room window peering out. Sue was in the kitchen, reclining on the counter, and Sugary was curled up and resting on the bed.

The lights were all out and the apartment was silent.

“Are you scared?” I said to Sugary.

“A little bit,” she said. “Are you?”

I started nodding. “A little bit,” I said. “In a scary situation, being scared is common sense.”

I checked out the night table right beside the bed: radio, alarm clock, telephone, lamp.

“Ms. Kitty said there aren’t any jewels in the bedroom. So the only thing he’s after is the Rumplemeyer, Sugary. Spike says it’s worth about 100 thousand bucks.”

“Are you trying to tell me he won’t come into the bedroom?”

“If he does,” I said soothingly, “he’ll rush in and out. Now you know what to do and you know when to do it.”

She nodded.

"Good luck."

From the white kitchen countertop, Sue whispered, *"Psst!"*

"You're fine," I said, "aren't you."

"Why are you assuming I'm fine?" she said testily. "Just because I'm level-headed, gutsy, and efficient, it doesn't mean I'm *fine.*"

I looked her in the eye. "You need support and reassurance."

"Darn right I do," she said.

I kept looking at her face. "I trust you more than anyone I know," I said warmly. "And I'd fight to the death to protect you — okay?"

"Are you serious?"

"Of course not," I said. "I say that to everyone." She stared for a second, then grinned, and then laughed.

In the living room, Spike was still sitting on the ledge. He looked at me somberly. "You think it's gonna work?"

I glanced at the Rumplemeyer, sitting on a shelf. We'd carefully removed it from its spot on the table — just far enough away so that Quark would have to waste a few minutes on the hunt.

I glanced at the stereo — a stack of components on the other side of the room.

I looked back at Spike and said . . . absolutely

nothing. I might have said, "Well, who knows?" or "Let's hope." But I opened my mouth and the sound that filled the living room was *Meow-Meow-Meow.*

The signal!

I suddenly streaked through the cat door and bounded to the roof.

24

A swift dark shadow moved among the shadows — a looming black lump among the canvas recliners and the tables and the chairs.

Quark paused briefly at the edge of the rooftop and peered into the night. He was medium height — slim and athletic in a black hooded sweatsuit. A black woolen ski mask was stretched across his face.

He looked like Batman. Batman about to take a long flying leap.

I watched as he stepped up smoothly to the ledge and then disappeared over it, black-gloved hands clinging lightly to the edge. The next thing I heard was the sound of his sneakers as he landed on the terrace and the muted click-scratch as his key opened the door.

I looked around quickly.

Angie and the Fangs were so beautifully hidden that I couldn't even see them. Then I saw Chang.

He was pacing back and forth on the television antenna like a tightrope walker who performed without a net.

I leapt to the ledge and began to do the countdown:

Five . . .

Four . . .

Three . . .

Two . . .

One . . .

Blast off!

The night split open with a thundering, shattering assault of rock'n'roll:

An attack of heavy metal from the night table radio, disco from the living room, punk from the kitchen, and an outraged objection from the woman next door:

"THAT DOES IT, YOUNG FELLA. I'M CALLING THE POLICE!"

I grinned. It was working. It was actually working.

The sound effects told me what was happening below.

Quark went into the bedroom and turned off the radio.

Then he ran to the kitchen and turned off the radio but just as he'd finished it — uh-oh! the radios blasted him again.

This time, he fled. This time I watched him as

he jumped to the terrace rail and then chinned himself to the roof.

I waited till his black-gloved hands hit the ledge and then I landed on his hands. I bit, but I only got the taste of black leather and the odor of his rage.

Besides, I'm no Rambo.

I backed off and crouched.

Quark came over the ledge. He was almost as terrific an acrobat as Chang. He chinned himself up and came over in a swift, neat, rapidly rolling somersault and rolled himself to his feet.

That's when he got it. From six sides at once.

Chang made a bomber-dive off the antenna and landed on Quark's shoulder.

Wang did a somersault and landed on his head.

Sturm, Drang and Angie hit his back, chest and arms, while I scrambled around his sneakers and untied the laces. Meanwhile, Butch, Jane and Oscar bit his legs.

He hollered and cursed. Threw Chang from his shoulder, kicked Oscar in the shin.

"Cover his eyes," I yelled to Wang.

Wang covered his eyes.

Quark, still cursing, stumbled blindly around the roof. He bumped into furniture. *Boom!* into a chair. *Crash!* into a table. *Boom-crash, boom-crash, boom-crash, boom!*

By now there were lights going on in all the

windows. People started hollering, "WHAT'S GOING ON?" and somewhere in the distance, a police siren wailed.

Quark struggled desperately attempting to get away but his struggling didn't pay. He tripped on his shoelace, hit an umbrella pole and knocked himself out.

He was flat on the ground.

At this point, a dozen of us landed on his stomach. The rock music thundered; the cop siren wailed.

I noticed the Rumplemeyer, lying unhurt in a small bed of flowers. And there, against the riot, it played a minuet.

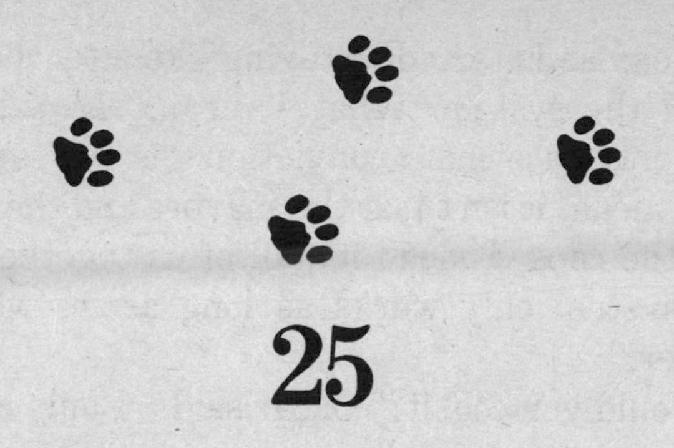

25

It was one of those wet-hot mornings in July when living in New York is like living in Brazil. There was shade in the courtyard — a big corner pocket that ran from the edge of my window to the gate — and we sat there, the veterans of last night's army, feeling slightly heroic and exceptionally brave.

"Final bulletin," I told them. "After Quark was arrested, the cops got a warrant and they checked his apartment and the jade was still there. Best of all," I said, grinning, "Mr. Crandle called Meany and Max was re-hired."

"Really nifty," Jane said. "I mean, you gotta admit it, guys. The system really works."

"Oh listen. Don't give me any slop about the system, man." Angie flicked her tail. "The system, man, didn't do nothin'. It was us."

"It was us *and* and the system." Spike cocked

his head and started lecturing like a teacher. "Or us *in* the system. What I mean," he said with suddenly passionate conviction, "is the system *is* us. I mean, it isn't just the mayors and the judges and the cops, I mean it's all of us together. And the system only works as long as *we* work together."

"Could you cool it?" Oscar said. "I only came to get some lox. I didn't come to get religion."

"And besides," Angie said, "I never once in my life met a group that stuck together. The way the world's goin', man, it's dog eat dog and every cat for himself."

Wang looked at Chang. "Did you ask her?"

"Not yet." Chang turned back to Angie. "We decided we're inviting you to join us," Chang said. "You got talent, kid. We figured we could use you in the act."

"Aw go on," Angie said.

Sue looked at her. "You know? We could wash and dry your hair. Add some highlights? A little curl? And I'd say if you lost about an ounce . . . you'd be a knockout."

"*Moi?*" Angie said.

"Where's the salmon?" Oscar said. "I only came to get some food. Where's Sugary?"

"I'm coming, coming, coming," Sugary said. She bounded across the courtyard. Butch was at her side. He was carrying a small plastic bag between his teeth. "This was heavy," Sugary said. "A half a pound of lox weighs at least half a pound."

Butch dropped the bag. "And there's some other stuff besides. Some canned stuff," he said.

Sue helped him open it. She unwrapped the lox and made a decorative platter while Sugary bubbled on:

"Did you tell them all?" she said. "Did you tell them how terrifically magnificent I was?"

"I sort of mentioned it," I said.

She turned around and faced the group. "I was terrifically magnificent. I turned on the radio, I hid under the covers, I turned it on again, and *then*" — she paused dramatically — "I telephoned the cops and then I howled into the phone. The cops said it sounded like a baby in distress. I was wonderful," she said.

Sue cocked her head. "Some of us," she purred and looked pleasantly at Angie, "need some extra self-esteem. And some of us," she said, looking cheerfully at Sugary, "could use a little less."

"Let's eat," Oscar said.

I looked at the lox spread carefully on the ground. I counted. Half a pound was exactly . . . eleven slices. And all I got to do was blink once and they were gone — everybody eating, going, *"Mmm, chomp, mmm."*

Okay, I thought begrudgingly. At least I get the can.

I squinted at the can.

CATSLOP, it said.

I went home and went to bed.

About the Author

Linda Stewart has written crime novels, television movies, and documentaries. She's been living with Sam since 1989 and keeping track of his adventures.